TRAPPED

Everyday Heroes Series Book Three

Margaret Daley

Trapped

Copyright © 2018 by Margaret Daley

a duplex was less than half an hour, but her twin sister had called her several hours ago and left a message. Since then, questions had raced through Sadie's mind. If only she'd been able to talk to Katie when she'd called. Sadie needed answers that would keep her growing panic at bay.

Something is wrong.

That was what she'd thought after listening to Katie's message. A desperate ring to her sister's voice had sent a shiver down Sadie's spine. Before leaving her house, she'd tried calling Katie back to find out what was going on, but her sister never answered.

Before Sadie lost cell reception, she drove onto the narrow shoulder of the road and made a final call to Katie. The continuous ringing of the landline at the cabin chilled her. She was twenty minutes away. A lot could happen in that time. She started to pull back onto the road when an idea struck her.

Brock Carrington—a next-door neighbor lived only minutes away from Katie.

For a few seconds, Sadie couldn't bring

2

ONE

Sadie Williams glanced up at the darkening clouds gathering in the sky above her. A few splashes of rain hit he windshield, and she hoped she'd arrive her twin's house before the heav opened up. A streak of lightning bright the growing darkness in the early p the afternoon.

While a stretch of straight r before her, she tightened her gri steering wheel and pushed her on the accelerator. She needed usual time to the large famil drive from Butte City, Col Sadie had recently returned herself to contact him. Scenes from their past flashed across her mind. Still, she didn't have a choice.

Her hand shook as she punched in the numbers she would never forget.

Again, though, there was no answer. But she knew Brock. He rarely left his home according to her sister.

An answering machine came on, and all she could do was leave a message. "Brock. This is Sadie. I think Katie's in trouble. Please check on her."

The second she finished, she pulled onto the road and pressed down on the gas pedal. She hoped to make up some time, but quickly the rain turned from sprinkles to a downpour. At least earlier, she'd stopped before heading up the side of a ten-thousand-foot mountain so that she could put up her top on her steel blue sports car.

She glimpsed the edge of the two-lane highway on her left and immediately returned her attention to the road before she went off the asphalt. But she couldn't get the sheer drop off, only a couple of feet from the right side of her sports car, out of her mind.

Thunder rumbled through the air. The loud noise shook her vehicle. As rain pelted the windshield quicker than the wipers could swipe it away, she leaned forward as though that would give her a clearer picture of what was before her. It didn't. She slowed her car. Her tension increased with each curve she had to take. Each one she went around, hopefully, drew her closer to answers about her sister.

When the log cabin came into view, its sight sent relief through her. In the dimness from the storm, she spied a light shining through the partially closed blinds of the living room. Her gaze skipped from one window to the next. Her family's "log cabin" had always been a haven for her. They used to come up here a couple of times a month before her father died from a heart attack and her mother left Denver for Arizona. Katie had moved into it to keep it maintained. The two-story house with three thousand square feet had been a second home for them.

Sadie drove down the paved driveway that circled in front of the cabin. She parked as close to the front entrance as possible. She should wait in her car until the intensity of the storm lessened, but she couldn't. What if Katie was hurt?

Sadie grabbed her waterproof jacket, shoved open the door, threw the light coat over her head, and ran the short distance to the shelter of the porch. She'd hoped Katie would open the door. But she didn't.

Sadie tried the knob. Locked. She dug into her purse and withdrew her copy of the cabin's key, which she'd always had on her although she hadn't been back here since Brock returned to his family home next door and lived there. When she inserted the key into the lock, she turned it and stepped into the foyer. The large living area before her was neat with everything in its right place—just how her sister liked it.

"Katie."

The shout rang through the silence.

Sadie shivered and glanced at the water dripping off her wet clothes onto the wooden floor. She moved to a throw rug a few feet away while yelling, "Katie, I'm here. Where are you?" She tried to tap down the fear growing in the pit of her stomach, but she couldn't.

She moved further into the cabin, crossing the room to the large fireplace and dropping her wet coat and purse onto the stones rather than the hardwood floor or furniture. Then she walked toward the kitchen, determined to search the house before totally panicking.

As she checked the room and even the pantry closet, nothing seemed out of place except a mug with a few sips of tea remaining sat next to the stainless-steel sink. If Katie had left the cabin, she would have cleaned and put up any dishes she'd used.

What if she was still here and hurt?

The question prodded Sadie forward, and she hurriedly went through the rest of the first floor—a library/office and bathroom. Then she headed up the stairs, her steps quickening as she moved from one bedroom to the next one. At the end of the hall where Katie stayed, she slowed her frantic pace.

Which was worse? Katie not here? Or her being in her bedroom, hurt or...?

She pivoted toward the entrance, fortifying herself with a deep breath and pushing into the bedroom. It looked exactly like it had when she visited her sister. She stepped inside and walked around then inspected the bathroom connected to the room. When she opened the closet door, her eyes widened

* * *

Brock Carrington pulled into his garage and turned off his engine, glad the rain was finally abating. Bella, his service dog, barked as she did every time they arrived home. He released Bella from her safety restraints. He did what he could to keep her protected because she'd brought him back from the edge after he returned to the United States from the war zone, a broken man. His life had fallen apart four years ago, but slowly he was rebuilding it.

Brock entered his house. A red light on

his landline phone indicated a message. He hurried to answer it in case it was one of the veterans from his coping group. The second he heard Sadie's voice, he tensed. He hadn't seen her in years, not since he'd broken off their engagement.

The words "I think Katie's in trouble" riveted his attention. His hand clutching the phone tightened. The fear he heard in her voice shook him.

Although he lived next door to Katie for the past three years, every time he saw her, he couldn't get Sadie out of his mind. The pain from their breakup had been too much to handle on top of dealing with PTSD and learning to live with a prosthetic leg from the knee down. Brock had avoided Katie as much as possible until recently as he'd put his life back together. He had to go over and make sure Katie was all right—and then let Sadie know.

His journey back from the edge of despair had tested him more than a firefight in Afghanistan, even the one that had taken a third of his squad out and left him close to death.

He grabbed his rifle in case there was trouble and headed for the front door, calling Bella. His golden retriever trotted next to him as he departed his home and trekked across the yard into the wooded area surrounding the Williams' family cabin. When he emerged from the grove, he spied two unfamiliar cars in front of Katie's place.

Brock patted his leg, indicating to Bella to stay by his side, and crept forward. Memories of his last skirmish as a U.S. Marine flooded his mind. Sweat popped out on his forehead, and his heartbeat increased.

* * *

Clothes and shoes littered the floor as though Sadie's sister frantically went through her wardrobe trying to decide what she should wear. A blank spot on the shelf above Sadie to the right drew her attention. Her sister's backpack was gone. Had Katie left willingly without telling Sadie? Or had she been forced to leave?

Had she driven away?

Katie had asthma and required an inhaler if triggered. Hopefully, she had it with her when she left.

Was her sister's car in the garage? She swiveled around and started for the hallway when she heard a squeak on the staircase. The sound stopped her in her tracks at the bedroom doorway. Someone was in the house? Katie?

Her sister knew Sadie's car and would have called out her name. What if whoever was coming up the stairs wasn't Katie? Sadie retreated to the closet near the entrance and pulled the door almost closed. Then she frantically looked around for a weapon she could use if it was an intruder. Where was a good baseball bat or a gun when she needed it?

Then Sadie spied a trophy her sister won years ago on the top shelf. Sadie climbed onto a stool Katie used when reaching for items up there and grabbed the hefty prize then moved to the narrow gap that afforded her a partial view of the bedroom.

Wearing a black ski mask, a tall, slender man, thin as a string bean, entered. Her heartbeat thudded against her skull. Her mouth went dry when she saw the guy's fingers wrapped around the handle of a gun. Her hand clutching her weapon shook as she lifted it in anticipation of the attacker checking the closet. The only thing she really had going for her was the element of surprise.

String Bean stopped a few feet from her, scanning the room. His shoulders tensed, and he began to lift his hand with the gun as he turned.

Sadie charged out of the closet, raising her arm and smashing the heavy trophy down on the side of his head, once then twice. He wavered then crumbled to the floor. She dropped her weapon, snatched his revolver from his grasp, and checked his pulse. Still breathing. Then she whirled, racing for the stairs.

As she headed down the staircase, questions flew through her mind. Who was that guy upstairs? Was he looking for Katie or something in her house? Where was her sister? If her car was gone, what did that mean? Did her sister leave knowing someone was coming after her? But what if the car was in the garage, then what happened to Katie?

She raced across the large living area and through the kitchen. In the utility room, she wrenched open the door into the garage and came to a halt as she stared at the empty space before her.

She didn't even know what to feel. Relief? Fear?

She needed to call the sheriff's office and then find something to tie up that guy until help arrived. Rope hung on the garage wall near the door, and she snatched it off its hook. She backed away. One of the landline phones was in the living room. She left the kitchen and started toward the desk. In three steps, she came to a halt.

Another man, short and stocky, also wearing a black ski mask, stood by the staircase. He lifted his shotgun. Although she held his partner's weapon, she hadn't used a gun before. Sadie twirled around and raced through the kitchen to the garage, banging her hand against the door opener.

TWO

Brock sneaked across Katie's porch with his dog at his side. What if she had visitors? Then he noticed the front door was ajar—not something she would do because she'd had a bear wander into her house the last time she did that. Bella growled, which made the hairs on the nape of Brock's neck rise. She didn't do that unless something was wrong.

His gut knotted as he slinked to the entrance and eased the gap wider. Silence. He started into the cabin when he heard the explosion of gunfire followed by the garage door going up. Bella began barking.

He whirled around and leaped off the

porch as he charged toward the right with Bella next to him. Katie—or was it Sadie—burst from the garage running as fast as she could. Her gray eyes wide, she looked right at him, and he knew it was Sadie.

She didn't slow down as she headed toward the two cars a few yards away. When she rounded the front of the SUV blocking the sports car from moving forward, Brock changed his direction and headed toward her. Bella didn't follow as usual. Instead his dog stood her ground, snarling. A man in a ski mask emerged from the garage, holding a shotgun.

"Bella, heel." Brock paused, making sure his golden retriever followed his direction as he lifted his rifle.

Bella obeyed the command.

The intruder brought up his weapon and fired it at Sadie, who had hunched down, using the SUV as a shield.

While Brock raced toward her as fast as he could with a prosthetic leg, he fired his gun.

The man ducked back into the garage.

Brock yanked the passenger door open to the sports car, knowing Sadie had always loved that kind of vehicle and signaled for Bella to jump in. Then he aimed his gun where the guy disappeared and released another shot, hoping to keep him penned down. Sadie hurried to her blue car and started the engine. But before he dove into the front passenger seat, he shot out a tire on the black SUV facing Sadie's vehicle.

As he shut the door, she put her vehicle in reverse and slammed her foot down on the accelerator while Brock, leaning out the passenger window, shot his rifle again at the garage. When Sadie reached the end of the circle, she turned onto the long driveway. The assailant stepped out of the garage and returned fire. The pellets peppered the back of her car. All color faded from Sadie's face as she clutched the steering wheel so hard her knuckles were white.

They approached the end of the highway.

"Which way?" she asked.

"Right. That's the quickest way to get help and report to the sheriff what happened."

She slowed to make the turn. "But I think Katie went left. I need to find her."

"It's possible that the sheriff can catch that guy if we call him as soon as possible."

Sadie jerked the steering wheel to the right then pressed the accelerator, taking the first curve as fast as she dared.

Brock glanced back to make sure no one was behind them and that Bella was okay. "What's going on? I just arrived home and got your message. Where's Katie? Is she okay?"

Shock and distress finally set in and warred for dominance on his ex-fiancée's face. He'd seen it before when she'd come into his hospital room at the base in Germany where he'd been flown from the war zone. He'd been shot while on a mission. She'd tried to act like his leg, amputated at the knee, didn't bother her, but the pity he saw in her eyes broke his heart. She'd denied it but—

"Katie's car's gone. It looks like she packed a bag. But something doesn't feel right. Her closet is a mess."

"Like a struggle took place?" He looked down at the car console.

"No. I think Katie did it in her haste to get away from here."

"Where did you get that handgun?" He gestured at the console. When he had known Sadie, she'd been unfamiliar with using weapons.

"With those two men who showed up with guns, I can see why Katie fled."

Brock's gaze fixed on her. "Two?"

"Yeah. I knocked out one in Katie's bedroom. I grabbed his gun and fled downstairs to see if her car was in the garage. That's when I discovered the other guy with the shotgun."

"What did she say to you when she alled?" He couldn't take his eyes off her. e hadn't seen her in years. At first, he'd en stayed away from Katie although they ere neighbors, but she was so different from Sadie, and he'd focused on their dissimilarities.

"I never talked to her. I got a message on my phone." For a few seconds, Sadie glanced at Bella in the back then returned her attention to Brock. "She wanted me to come see her. I just moved to Butte City a few days ago and live in a duplex. She needed to talk to me but didn't want to say anything over the phone. Although she didn't say something was wrong, I could hear it in her voice. I know Katie, and she sounded scared."

"How long ago was that?" He hadn't known that Sadie had returned to Colorado. Katie never said anything to him about it, but after he broke off his engagement to Sadie, he'd been in a bad place. Was that why Katie had called early in the week and asked him over to dinner tonight? To break the news that Sadie was here?

"Almost three hours ago. On the drive up the mountain before cell reception faded, I tried to call her. She didn't answer. I never saw her car go by me."

"She might have gone up the mountain and down the other side, or she left right after she called you. It only takes thirty minutes to go down this side."

"Then why did she leave after asking me to come to the house?"

The confused, stunned expression on her face twisted his gut. Katie and Sadie were twins and on the surface looked exactly alike. The sisters were close but had very different personalities. Sadie loved books, the written word, and cooking while Katie loved numbers and statistics. Sadie was a crusader while her twin only wanted to be behind the scenes. Sadie was an extrovert. Katie was an introvert. That was why they never tried to swap places and pretend to be the other one in school. "Did you call her cell phone as well as her landline?"

"Yes, but the phones went to voicemail. I've left several messages, but as long as she's on the mountain, she won't get them."

Brock faced forward. "After we report

the break-in to the sheriff, we can search for Katie. She could have gone to her office. The last few days she's been upset about something. I thought that was why she wanted me to come over for dinner tonight."

Sadie pulled off the highway into a small paved area where others often did before leaving cell reception. She picked up her phone in a cup holder. "I'm trying Katie's cell to see if she'll answer now."

"While you do that, I'll call Clay. He's the sheriff now." In order to give her privacy, Brock slipped from the front seat and walked a few paces away from the car while he talked to Clay Maxwell. They had grown up together in Butte City.

When the sheriff answered, Brock said, "There's been a break-in at Katie Williams' house on the mountain. Two men—one had a shotgun and the other a handgun. Katie wasn't at the house, but Sadie was because her sister called her upset. When she knocked out one of the intruders, Sadie took the handgun and ran. It's in her car."

"How did the men get to the cabin?"

"In a black SUV. I shot out two of the tires to delay them."

"Any license plate numbers."

"Although I noticed a Chevy logo on the SUV, all I saw on the front license plate was seventy-five at the end. I didn't have much time with the guy shooting at us."

"Just a moment."

While Clay put him on hold, Brock looked into the car. Sadie rested her forehead against the steering wheel. She straightened and glanced at him.

The sheriff came back on the line. Brock looked away. Being close to Sadie again after four years played havoc with his emotions. Right now, he needed to remain focused on what happened at the Williams' cabin.

"Two deputies are headed toward the cabin. One from each side of the mountain. The deputy on the other side is nearby and should reach the cabin soon. Both of them will be on the lookout for a black SUV. Where are you and Sadie?"

Brock turned away from the car—away from Sadie. "At the cell reception pullover on the east side of the mountain."

"Stay where you are until I tell you one of my officers is at the place. When it's safe, I'll let you know, and you two can come back to the cabin. I'll be there shortly."

"Okay. We will." Brock pocketed his cell phone, his back still to her as he moved to the rear of her car to keep an eye out for the black SUV.

He knew Sadie well. She would insist on going to look for Katie. When she was on a mission, nothing deterred her from her goal. That had been something he admired about her—her focus and determination. And in this case, he couldn't blame her for wanting to do that. The twins were very different but also very close.

He looked down and glimpsed several bullet holes in her trunk, a reminder of the dangerous situation Sadie had been in. What if he had returned home later and found her injured or dead at Katie's? If that had happened—

He shoved that question from his mind.

For a moment, he needed to remain where he was while he wrestled with his past memories—especially the day he broke off their engagement and now this.

* * *

Sadie, trying to relax her tense muscles, leaned back against her seat. She pried her fingers from the steering wheel and fisted her hands then uncurled them. When she'd called Brock earlier and left a message about Katie, she'd known there would be a good chance she would see him again after the day she'd walked out of his hospital room where he'd told her he didn't want to marry her.

She could picture the scene as though it was happening right now in front of her. She placed her engagement ring on the table beside his bed then looked at him, hoping he really hadn't meant he didn't want to be with her anymore. But he'd turned away from her, staring at one of his monitors. Tears blurred her vision. She'd told him she didn't care he'd lost a leg. The words meant nothing to him.

She'd pivoted and walked away from him. At the door, she stopped and glanced back to appeal to him. The coldness she'd seen in his face had frozen her heart. When he left the hospital in Germany and came back to the United States, she'd waited weeks for him to change his mind. He hadn't. He wouldn't accept her calls, in fact, he took no one's. It took her months finally to realize the only way she was going to make it was to stay away from him and put the country between them.

A cold nose nudged her. She glanced over her shoulder into the golden retriever's face. Something in the golden retriever's brown eyes made Sadie wonder if the dog could read her mind. Bella tilted her head and laid it against Sadie's shoulder. This connection to the canine jammed her throat with a tight wad of emotions. Four years ago, she'd cried until there was nothing left inside her. She wouldn't do that again. Brock and she had been so close, having known each other from their teenage years. She didn't understand why he sent her away. They had been best friends before they fell in love. Now they were strangers.

Brock opened the passenger's door and slid into the front seat. His presence filled the small car. His black hair was cut short as though he were still a solider. His intense dark brown eyes connected with hers.

She looked away and swallowed hard. She had to toughen her heart to what could have been. That was the past. It couldn't be changed. Her motto had always been to live for the present—not the past or future.

He stared out the windshield. "The sheriff just called. A deputy is at the cabin. The SUV is gone. Clay wants us to go back to Katie's. He'll be there probably before us."

"Was that why you were looking at the highway? To see if the two guys went by here?"

"Yes. They didn't."

"Then they must have gone over the mountain and down the west side." Which was the direction she thought Katie had gone. Had those two assailants found her sister yet?

"Maybe. But the deputy came that way and didn't see a black SUV."

"Then they probably turned off the road. Possibly they ditched their car and got a new one." She started the engine and turned the vehicle around then pulled onto the highway. "At least it isn't raining anymore."

"And the temperature is still above freezing. In spring, it can change fast. I hope it stays dry, and the weather report is wrong."

"Why?"

"There's a big storm with strong winds moving this way. If the temperature drops, that means a possible blizzard."

"When?"

"If it slows down, possibly three or four

days."

"And if it doesn't?"

"Tomorrow. Let's hope the rain or snow disappears from the forecast although it has been dry for the past couple of months."

Again, Sadie pushed the speed as fast as she could without going off the cliff. "I have to find Katie before that. Bad weather can only make it harder."

"And you don't have any idea why she could be in trouble?"

Sadie shook her head. "But we haven't talked much since I moved back here. I had a deadline for my new cookbook. I shouldn't have picked the time while my book was due to my publisher to move. I thought I could get it done before the deadline, but packing requires more time than I realized."

"Why not just wait?"

"Because a couple wanted to buy my house and move into it right away. I couldn't say no to that. Once I was at my new duplex, I dug in, living out of two boxes for three days. I emailed my book off last night and started to unpack some of my belonging this morning."

"That doesn't surprise me. You always turned assignments in on time."

"That's one thing Katie and I have in common." She rounded a curve and slammed on the brakes when a deer raced across the highway. Her car fishtailed as the animal disappeared into the thick trees. She glanced at Brock.

He gripped the door handle and the side of the seat."I see your driving hasn't improved. It won't do Katie any good if we end up in a wreck."

Frowning, she slowed her speed. "I haven't had a wreck in a long time. I forgot how often animals cross this road unexpectedly. This is the first time I've been to the cabin in years." Because she hadn't wanted to come to the cabin and remember all the fond memories from her past with Brock—not until she thought she'd put her life back together after Brock ended their engagement. Now she wasn't so sure she really had.

Silence reigned for a few minutes before Brock asked, "When Katie told me about your two cookbooks, I didn't believe it. I thought she was joking. You never particularly liked cooking. What happened?"

After they broke up, cooking had become calming and comforting for her. It quickly turned to a passion, starting with a podcast that showed her journey from a person who could barely prepare a dish to an accomplished cook. Over the years, the viewers of her podcasts grew and encouraged her. "True. But life is full of changes, as we both know." The last few words came out before she had a chance to censor them. No matter what happened to them four years ago, Brock went through more changes than she ever had.

Quiet returned, and she wasn't about to break it. Despite their past, she felt safer with Brock nearby. She had always felt that way. That hadn't changed, although a lot of other things had since they parted ways.

As she turned onto Katie's long

driveway, Sadie spied two sheriff's cars in front of the cabin. "I hope they've found my sister and the two intruders."

"So do I." Brock sat forward scanning the terrain around the house. When she parked behind the sheriff's vehicle, Brock quickly exited her car and pushed the front seat forward for his golden retriever to hop out of the two-door vehicle.

As Sadie scrambled from the driver's seat, Brock started toward the woods that stood between their property. "Where are you going?"

"My place. Lights are on, and I didn't turn them on."

THREE

Brock pointed to Sadie. "Go inside with the deputy. Clay will be here soon. Bella, guard." His golden retriever trotted to Sadie.

"Don't go over there alone." She pivoted toward his house.

"I'll be fine. You should go inside. We don't know what's going on." Brock raised his arm with the rifle clutched in his hand and started toward his place at a lope.

Sadie, with Bella, stepped up onto the cabin's porch and glanced over her shoulder.

Brock increased his pace the closer she approached her front door. When she disappeared inside, he increased his pace. He couldn't think of anyone who would be at his place. There was no car parked nearby. With what happened at Katie's this morning, he had to be vigilant. Something wasn't right.

Katie had seemed worried the last time he'd seen her. Usually she told him about what was going on at work and her personal life. Instead, he'd had to fill the void in the conversation—as though their roles had been reversed. He should have pressed her, but when he didn't want to talk about something, Katie always respected his privacy.

As he approached his home, he peeked into the window, hoping he could assess the situation before going inside. But he didn't see anything unusual. Could he have left the lights on when he went over to Katie's earlier? It had been raining, and the sky was darker than usual because of the storm system. As he headed for the entrance, he replayed what he'd done after he heard the message Sadie left on his phone. He'd flipped on one light, but he'd also turned it off when he left.

Which meant someone was inside.

He unlocked his front door and stealthy crept into the entry hall. The light was coming from the kitchen. As he sneaked toward the room and pressed himself against the wall near the entrance, he heard the sound of a cabinet door closing. He raised his rifle and swung into the entry. He latched onto the sight of the back of a man about six feet tall with long brown hair. He moved to the refrigerator.

Brock kept his weapon aimed at the intruder. "Why are you here?"

* * *

Sadie stepped into the living room, stunned while she scanned the clutter that must have been created by the intruders after she and Brock left.

A deputy sheriff descended the staircase. "I'm Sadie Williams. Katie, who lives here, is my twin sister."

"I'm Deputy Adams. The sheriff will be here soon. I just called him to let him know the extent of the mess."

"When we left earlier, this area," she swept her arm in a wide arc, "wasn't trashed like this. Is the upstairs trashed, too, other than my sister's bedroom closet?"

"No, ma'am." Deputy Adams crossed the wide room to her.

What were those two men looking for to take time to do this after she and Brock left? Must be important. Surely, the intruders would consider they would call the sheriff.

"Ms. Williams, do you have any idea what they were after?"

She shook her head while glancing at her watch—three-fifteen.

"Can you describe the two men?"

"Other than one was tall and thin while the other was stocky and short, no. They wore black ski masks."

"What color were their eyes?"

For a long moment, she replayed what transpired earlier. "I don't remember. I hit the one over his head in my sister's room. It knocked him out. I checked his pulse. He was alive when I ran out into the hallway. When I encountered the second intruder, I was coming out of the kitchen. He was across the living room. I saw his gun and reacted without really looking at his covered face or his eyes. I ran for the garage."

"I understand Brock Carrington was with you."

What was taking Brock so long?"Yes, but he noticed a light coming from his house. He went to check it out."

The front door opened, and Sheriff Clay Maxwell entered. Sadie had gone to school with him. Like Brock, Clay was a couple of years older. "Where's Brock?

She explained. "Please go check on him."

"I will. Deputy Adams stay with Ms. Williams."

"Yes, sir."

"Clay, I'd like to go with you." The words came out of her mouth without her thinking it through.

"No." The sheriff turned and exited the cabin.

That left Sadie to fret about Brock. What if the two assailants she'd encountered were at his house earlier? They could be part of a robbery ring. But she hadn't seen their SUV in front of Brock's place. They might have hidden it after what happened here. In fact, that would have been a good idea for them since they would probably think she would call the sheriff and give him the description of the getaway car. Her mind raced with all kinds of possibilities.

"Does it look like anything was stolen?" the deputy asked.

"I haven't been here recently, so I don't know. My sister will have to tell you that. Has anyone found her yet?"

"No, nor her car."

Sadie paced, chewing on her thumbnail. What if something happened to Brock because of her? She shouldn't have called him earlier.

* * *

Brock lowered his rifle as the man turned

37

toward him. "What are you doing here, Simon?"

His younger brother drew in a deep breath then released it. "I wanted to visit you. I haven't seen you in months. You need to work on your hospitality skills."

While trying to calm his fast heartbeat, Brock set his weapon on the counter nearby. "You always let me know ahead of time. This isn't a good time to spring a surprise visit on me. I thought you were an intruder."

"Sorry. I didn't want to give you a chance to say no."

Brock cut the distance to his brother. "You should be at the university finishing your master's degree." He was glad to see his brother but not at this time, especially if something was going on with Katie. When his dad died seven years ago, he promised to look out for Simon.

"I've been working on my thesis a lot. I needed a break."

"How did you get here? I didn't see your car."

"I traded my Chevy for a Harley. I

brought it into your garage."

"It's still not a good time." And especially riding a motorcycle up the mountain when it was pouring down rain. He'd lost too many people to have his brother act recklessly. But saying anything to Simon wouldn't change him, so Brock clamped his jaw closed.

"Why? What's going on? I saw a deputy sheriff's car outside Katie's house. Has something happened? Is that where you've been?"

"Yes. But it's nothing you need to be concerned about."

Simon hiked his chin up. "Ah, there you go into your protective big brother mode. This is our family home. I have a right to stay here."

Brock gritted his teeth, trying to remain calm. "I'm the one who poured my money into fixing up this place. You're living in our home in Denver. You could have taken a break at your house there, so what's really going on?"

"Lexie and I broke up. I needed to get out of town."

"Who did the breaking up—you or her?"

"Lexie. I didn't see it coming. I don't know what to do. I love her, and I thought she loved me. Any advice?"

The doorbell rang, giving Brock a reprieve from answering his brother. He hurried from the kitchen. How could he give Simon advice on love? He hadn't been successful in his own love life.

When he opened the door, he was relieved to see his best friend, Clay.

"Is everything all right? Sadie was worried about a possible intruder at your place." The sheriff looked beyond Brock. "Nice to see you, Simon."

Brock glanced back at his brother. "On impulse, Simon decided to pay me a visit without letting me know. I'll walk back to Katie's house with you, Clay."

Simon approached Brock. "I'll come, too. Why didn't you tell me Sadie's here? What happened at Katie's?"

"That's what we're trying to find out." Brock was only going to answer his little brother's last question. Brock left his place last and locked the door. "Any news on the black SUV?"

"A couple of leads but nothing's panned out yet. Someone really made a mess at Katie's house."

Brock came to a halt next to Simon and stared at Clay. "What do you mean? Sadie said everything was where it should be except in Katie's bedroom closet."

"The living room was trashed. They must have been looking for something."

"How was the rest of the place?" Brock asked, noting another sheriff's vehicle parked behind the other two.

"I don't know yet. I came over to make sure you were okay. She was worried. Where's the intruder's handgun Sadie took?"

"It's locked in her car on the console."

"Good. I'll get it when I leave."

Brock mounted the steps to the porch, and the front door swung open.

Deputy Morris exited the house. "A black SUV was sighted on the highway on the west side speeding back up the mountain. We're going to trap him between us."

Clay waved his hand."Go. Let me know what happens."

Some of the tension in Brock siphoned from him. Since he'd heard Sadie's message on his phone, a knot in his gut had formed and tightened the longer it took to find her sister. A couple of years ago, he wouldn't have been able to deal with the stress. Now, thanks to the Lord, Bella, therapy, his determination, and the support group he formed to help others with PTSD, he'd been able to manage his anxiety.

When Brock followed the sheriff into the house, his gaze immediately went to Sadie standing in the middle of the chaos the intruders had caused in a short amount of time. Bella, alert to everything around her, sat right next to Sadie.

Simon paused beside Brock. "Why didn't you say something about Sadie returning? And this time, I want an answer," he whispered.

"She's been back only a few days, and I don't owe you an explanation." Brock stepped forward several feet before his brother continued his questions. He needed to focus on Sadie and help her. He owed her and Katie that much.

Sadie panned the destruction. Her shoulders sagged. Her dark red hair and gray eyes stood out against the pallor of her face. He wanted to comfort her, but he wasn't sure how. He knew how to support the men in his group, but his past with Sadie now stood in his way.

While Clay talked with Deputy Adams, her gaze caught Brock's and held it. He took another step toward her then again until he was standing in front of her. He started to grasp her hand but stopped. "Can I help you?"

"I have to find Katie. I don't want to call Mom and tell her Katie's disappeared. She fell apart when Dad died and is only now putting her life back together."

"I'll do whatever I can to help. And when Clay says it's okay, we'll clean this up."

Sadie scanned the chaos all around her. "What were they looking for? I can't see them taking the time to trash the place unless they had a good reason to do it."

"I agree. Except for the call this morning, has Katie indicated to you anything was wrong before today?"

Sadie tilted her head to the side and stared into space for a long moment. "Now that I think about it, two days ago she was supposed to meet me for lunch but called at the last moment and said she couldn't. I started to ask her what came up, but she ended the call before I could. I know at times she gets super busy with work, and I thought this was one of those times. But that might not be the reason."

Clay's radio squawked, and he stepped into the kitchen to answer the call.

Sadie leaned toward Brock and whispered, "I hope they've got the two guys."

The scent of vanilla that she often wore attacked his senses, and for a few seconds, he was transported to the past. That fragrance instantly reminded him of the times he'd kissed Sadie and had become lost in the sensations she created in him.

Clay returned to the living room. "Deputy Morris found an abandoned black

SUV off the highway. We're running the license plate to see who owns the car."

Sadie's eyelids closed for a few seconds. Then she looked right into Brock's eyes. "Maybe we'll get some answers."

"At least it's a start." This was the first glimpse of hope he'd seen in Sadie—in years. He didn't want to tell her that there was a good chance the vehicle had been stolen if it was now abandoned.

"Have you taken photos down here of the damage?" Clay asked his deputy.

"Yes, sir."

"How about upstairs?"

"Not yet, but I'll do it right now." Adams crossed to the staircase and headed for the second floor.

"While he does that, I'm going to see what I can find outside, especially in the garage. Sadie, I need the key to your car, so I can get the intruder's handgun. We might find something on it to help us."

"Sure." She retrieved her car key from her pocket and gave it to Clay.

"Thanks." The sheriff walked toward the door off the kitchen.

"Can we start cleaning up?" Brock asked Clay.

"Yes."

Sadie inhaled a deep breath. "I'd better get a trash bag to put the broken pieces in."

"I can get it," Simon said. "Anything to help."

"Thanks, Simon, but I know where they are." Sadie turned away but not before Brock saw the tears in her eyes.

His first urge was to reach out and draw her to him, but he hesitated a few seconds. She disappeared into the kitchen with Bella next to her.

Move. She needs comfort. Remember what you've learned. The past can't be changed. Don't live in it.

Brock went after Sadie. They had been really close once. He couldn't turn away from her in her time of need. In the kitchen, her back was to him. He clasped her shoulders. "You aren't alone. I want to help you. We'll figure out what's going on and find Katie. She could walk in at any moment."

She swung around, wet tracks coursing down her cheeks. "Do you really believe that after what's happened today?"

He couldn't lie to her. "It's not likely but not impossible. Something occurred here. That's for sure, but what if those two were really thieves, targeting the place, not Katie."

Sadie shook her head and splayed her hand over her heart. "In here, I know she's in trouble."

He'd marveled at the close relationship Sadie and Katie had. They usually knew when the other needed help. He cupped her face and ran his thumbs across her cheeks to wipe all traces of her tears away. "Then that's how we'll proceed and make that clear to Clay."

"Thanks for coming over. If you hadn't, I don't know if I'd been able to get away from that guy coming out of the garage."

"I'm glad I got there in time." He dropped his hands away from her face, immediately missing the warm connection between them. He snatched up the tall trashcan. "Let's clean up this place before

Katie returns."

"That's being optimistic. I was usually the one who believed everything would turn out fine."

"I've learned to change how I look at life. It took a while for this stubborn brain of mine to get the point that Pastor John was trying to tell me."

"Who is he?"

Pastor John dragged him kicking and screaming from that dark place he'd gone. "He runs a support group for veterans with PTSD. He's the reason I have Bella."

Sadie looked at his golden retriever at her side, her big brown eyes staring up at her. Sadie stooped down and rubbed Bella then hugged her. "I can see why you have her. She stayed next to me after you left to check on your house. Was everything all right over there?"

"Yes. Simon's visit wasn't on my schedule." Brock grinned. "But I shouldn't be surprised that he showed up unexpectedly. If he gets something in his head to do it, he usually does. Kind of reminds me of you."

"So that's why I like Simon." Sadie straightened and started toward the living room. "Until he came with you and Clay, I hadn't seen him in years. How long is he staying?"

"We didn't get to that. Clay showed up to see if I was all right." As he walked out of the kitchen, the door to the garage opened behind him, and the sheriff entered, a solemn expression on his face. Brock turned toward him. "What's happened?"

"I'm ninety-nine percent sure the black SUV my deputy found off the highway is the one the intruders used. The license plate ended in seventy-five."

"Good. Was it stolen?" Sadie asked as she came back to the entrance into the kitchen.

"I think so. We checked the license plate number for the person who owned the SUV. Tom Connors lives down the road off the highway from where the SUV was ditched. Deputy Morris went to talk to the guy. He discovered the door standing open and Connors' dead body in the entry hall.

The place was trashed like Katie's."

Her eyes grew round. Sadie put her fingers against her lips. He was Katie's supervisor at Mason and Fox Shipping.

FOUR

Had Sadie heard the sheriff right? "Tom Connors is dead?"

"Yes. Did you know him?" Clay asked, starting to move toward the foyer.

Sadie followed with Bella and Brock. "He is—was—Katie's supervisor at Mason and Fox Shipping. He oversaw the financial department. If the same two men are after my sister, then we have to find Katie before they do. There must be a connection somehow between Mr. Connors' death and Katie's intruders this morning."

Clay opened the front door.

Brock hurried around Sadie and blocked the sheriff's exit from the house. "We need to come with you. I know it isn't kosher, but Bella can track a person. She might be able to follow the two men's scent from the SUV and figure out how the guys got away from where they ditched the vehicle."

Clay glanced at Bella then back at Brock. "Only if you do exactly what I tell you."

"Of course, I will." Brock opened the door. "We'll follow you."

"We?"

"Yes. Sadie and Bella."

Clay frowned. "You should stay here, Sadie."

She'd been friends with the sheriff as long as Brock had. She had no problem using that past friendship. "Clay, I'm coming with you two. I know you have a deputy here, but I can't stay by myself. What if those men haven't found Katie? I look exactly like her." She grinned.

"But Simon will be here besides my deputy. That's two guards." Clay rubbed his hand along his chin.

"And don't forget the help, Clay, I gave you when you wanted to ask Haley to the prom."

The sheriff groaned. "Okay. But you'll be in the back of my squad car if you don't follow my directions."

Her eyes widened. "You'd arrest me?"

Clay let Deputy Adams know where they were going and ordered the deputy and Simon to stay at the house. "Let's go," the sheriff said then left the house first.

"Thanks." Sadie hurried to the driver's side of her vehicle while Brock let Bella hop into the back then slid into the front passenger's seat.

"I didn't know you set Clay up with Haley."

"It was easy. She'd been interested in him for weeks."

Brock chuckled. "And now they're married with two kids."

"Matchmaking is one of my hidden talents." Too bad her matchmaking skills hadn't worked on herself. Sadie started her sports car. "I didn't know Bella can track. Did you train her?"

"No. When I got her, she already knew how. I was lucky to find her. A veteran in a group I was in knew this guy who had several dogs he'd trained for service people who needed them. Bella had been well trained in search and rescues, but her instinct was also amazing as a companion. It was like she felt my internal pain. Whenever I was depressed or sad, she was right there to comfort me. In the past year, I continued Bella's training in search and rescue. We've helped in nine searches. It's a good feeling when you find the victim."

Sadie's grip on the steering wheel tightened. Brock never gave her a chance to be there for him. She would have been. She'd loved him and wanted to be his wife. As she pulled onto the highway behind Clay's vehicle, she slid a glance at Brock. He stared at her. She quickly returned her attention to the road.

"I'm sorry," Brock murmured in the thick silence.

"For what?"

"For not giving you a chance four years ago. I wasn't in a good place for a long time."

"But I could have helped you." Finally,

the words she'd wanted to say to him for years came out in a near whisper.

"I don't know if I would have heard you. I wasn't listening to anyone at that time. I didn't get Bella until a year later when I hit rock bottom. In the firefight I was injured in, a lot of my buddies were hurt or killed. There was nothing I could do to change that outcome."

Sadie had never been in a threatening situation until this morning in Katie's bedroom. Her reaction had even taken her by surprise, but she was glad she had fought back. She hadn't realized she had it in her. She parked on the side of the road behind the sheriff, at a loss as to what she should say to Brock. She parked and started to open the door but stopped and looked at him. "I wish that had never happened to you. I didn't get to tell you that. I wanted to be there for you."

"But I couldn't deal with it. You didn't deserve that from me." He pushed his door open and climbed from her car.

He let Bella out.

Sadie exited, too, her emotions shut

down. She couldn't go back and change the past. Right now, all she could do was try to find her sister and pray she was still alive. Clay pointed in the direction where the SUV had been ditched on the highway about a fourth of a mile from Connors' house. They walked to the abandoned black SUV.

"Do you two think this was the car?" the sheriff asked.

Sadie looked at it. "I didn't pay attention, so I can't say one way or another."

Brock and Bella circled the vehicle with Brock pausing at the front of it. When he returned, he nodded. "There's an indentation in the bumper that's the same as the one I saw when I fired at the car."

"Then that confirms the two intruders at Katie's are persons of interest in the death of Tom Connors. According to the deputy at Connors' house, there's a blood trail up his steps to the porch and inside." Clay gestured at his patrol car. "Let's go to the crime scene then come back to see if we can track where the two suspects went. Most likely, they got into the car they used to drive to Connors'.."

Clay drove to Katie's supervisor's house, set back from the road, and parked in front. When Brock and she climbed from the sheriff's vehicle, Clay pointed to the blood-stained steps and the wooden planks near the door on the porch. "Tom Connors might have interrupted the two men stealing his SUV, and they killed him, or it's something much more complicated."

"Like they were sent to kill him. If that were the case, then why?" Brock stared at the blood drops. "However it happened, Connors and Katie are connected. Why did they kill him then go after Katie?"

Clay mounted the four steps and stared through the screen door. "I wonder if Connors called Katie somehow and warned her. He wouldn't have necessarily died right away from his wound. It looks like he dragged himself inside. He wasn't far from his house phone."

When the sheriff opened the door to go inside, Brock glimpsed through the front entrance to where Connors' body laid with the deputy nearby. "If he didn't call 9-1-1, then who did he call? Katie?"

Sadie shook her head. "If he had called Katie, she would have said something to me when she left me the message, and she would have phoned 9-1-1 to report what happened to Connors. No. It was someone else."

"I'll be contacting the phone company to see what numbers Connors called this morning." Clay paused in the doorway. "While I walk through the crime scene, I need you to see if Bella can pick up the driver's scent in the SUV. Deputy Olson is processing the driver's side door for fingerprints before he opens it for Bella to smell. I don't want any possible evidence disturbed."

As Sadie walked with Brock to the black SUV near her car along the highway, more deputies arrived to process the crime scene at the house. The thought of the horrific scene described brought back her worry about her sister. Where was she? Had the two men found her and taken her out like her supervisor? Why? What was the connection? Tension pounded against her temples. The unknown was adding to her anxiety.

You aren't alone. I'm with you. Worrying is useless. It won't change anything. Keep your focus on Me.

She knew she shouldn't worry like she was. It wasn't helping the situation. *But, Lord, it's hard not to in this situation.*

While Bella smelled the driver's seat then began moving away from the SUV parked off the highway, Sadie paused for a moment, closed her eyes, and recited part of Psalm 24. *Yea, though I walk through the valley of the shadow of death, I will fear no evil: for thou art with me; thy rod and thy staff, they comfort me.*

She repeated those lines as she covered the space between her and Brock with Bella in thick brush and trees at the edge of the highway.

Brock glanced toward her. "There are tire tracks here and two faint set of footprints, most likely two men. They must have gotten into another car." He backed away from the area. "I need to tell Clay. Then we should leave. It'll take a while to process the murder scene."

Murder scene. The thought there could be one for her sister shivered down her spine. "I don't know what to do next. I should stay at Katie's in case she calls or comes back."

"No, you can't!"

"You can't tell me what I should do." She lifted her chin and narrowed her eyes. "You lost that privilege four years ago."

"You think that's what I'm doing?" He closed the space between them. "I'm trying to protect you. If you stay at Katie's house, you're putting yourself in danger. She didn't even want to stay. She left because she thought staying was dangerous. Whoever is after her, could think you're her. If something happened to you, how will that help Katie?"

* * *

In Brock's garage an hour later, he followed Simon and Sadie into his home—a furious Sadie who didn't like the question he'd asked about Katie or the fact they couldn't stay at her sister's house. Sadie charged through the kitchen and into the dining room to the window that faced Katie's place. He leaned down and stroked Bella. As much as he loved his dog, right now Sadie needed her more than he did.

"Guard," he whispered close to his golden retriever then pointed at Sadie.

As Bella trotted to her, Brock dragged a chair from the table to where Sadie stood. "At least you can sit while you keep an eye on your family home."

She glanced at Bella, her expression softening a bit. His dog sat next to Sadie who laid a hand on top of her head while she kept her gaze trained on the house a hundred yards away.

He stood behind her, looking out the window over her shoulder. All he saw was semi-darkness as the dusk settled over the terrain. "Are you going to stay there all night?"

"Yes. I'm glad the deputy turned all the lights off when he left. If the assailants come back to Katie's, I might see a light in the house. They can't search in the dark."

She sat in the chair. "I have to do something to find my sister. Tonight, this is it."

"And tomorrow?"

"I'll do what I can. I can't sit around doing nothing. I know Katie's in danger. I can feel it."

"I asked Clay to search for Katie's car. Hopefully, something will help us there."

She looked over her shoulder. "Thanks for thinking of that." She massaged her temple. "I should have thought about that."

"You've been focused on Katie. A lot has happened today."

Her shoulders sagged. "I still don't know why anyone would want to come after my sister."

"Same here but someone is."

"Sadie?" Simon asked behind Brock.

She leaned to the left. "I appreciate you helping Deputy Adams."

Simon looked at Sadie. "I'm sorry we couldn't find anything in the house to indicate where your sister could be. I'm glad you're staying here."

She smiled at Simon. "It's been a long

time since I saw you last. At Katie's we didn't have a chance to talk."

"Good. We can catch up on the past four years." Simon headed for the kitchen. "I'll fix something for dinner. Unless something has happened in the past couple of months, my big brother doesn't cook beyond making sandwiches or heating up a microwave dinner. I brought a few food items, so we won't starve."

Brock frowned. "On your motorcycle?"

At the entrance into the kitchen, Simon chuckled. "My motorcycle has a storage compartment I can use for groceries or anything I want to transport." He disappeared into the room.

"I see nothing has changed between you two." Sadie kept her gaze trained on her sister's house.

"Simon and I have our differences. Every few months, he invades my space. His reason is he has to escape the grind of getting his master's degree." Brock leaned toward Sadie and lowered his voice as he said, "But I know he was really worried about me those first two years when I returned to live here after my hospital and rehab stay. He wants to make sure I don't backslide."

Simon came to the doorway with a spatula in his hand. "And my big brother has been doing great even if he loves living by himself in the woods. Like a hermit."

Brock shook his head. "I like the quiet, the peace." He started toward Simon. "I hope you aren't fixing anything fancy. The last time you prepared some French dish that was way too rich for my palate."

"Unless it's meat and potatoes just about everything is too rich for you, so I'm making fried chicken with mashed potatoes and green beans to add a little color to your food."

Sadie gasped. She shot up to a standing position, leaned closer to the window, then pivoted so fast the chair she'd sat in toppled over. "Someone's at Katie's."

Brock flipped off the overhead light and came to Sadie's side. "Where?"

She tapped the glass, pointing to the rear of the house. "It's not totally dark yet, and I'm sure I saw a shadow move toward Katie's place. I'm going over there whether you come or not." She turned and took several steps. "It could be Katie."

"Or one of the intruders since the deputy's gone." Brock grasped her arm. "No. I won't let you. I'll go by myself."

Her steel-hard gaze met his. "I'm going with or without you."

He released a long breath. He wasn't going to change her mind. "Then wait until I can get my rifle and a flashlight in case we need either one."

Relief flickered in her eyes. "Thanks. I would feel safer if you did come."

When he'd come into his house, he'd left his rifle in the kitchen. "Let's go out the garage. Come, Bella." His dog, who had stayed at Sadie's side, barked. "We're going to Katie's." Another yelp accompanied that announcement.

"She understands where she's going?"

"Yes. We usually visit Katie once or twice a week." Brock withdrew a set of night vision binoculars and a flashlight from a kitchen drawer near the door to the garage.

"And yet Katie never gave you a clue to what could have caused this?"

"No, but then I haven't talked to her in several days."

"So, something could have happened during that time."

"Maybe." Brock looked at the counter by the stove. "Simon, we're going to Katie's to check out the place. You might wait before frying that chicken."

"Do you need me to come?" His brother turned off the burner and removed a frying pan full of cooking oil.

"No. Make sure all the doors stay locked." Brock picked up his rifle and opened the door. As he and Sadie stepped into the garage, he added, "Please stay behind me no matter what you see. Okay?"

"Yes," she answered after a slight hesitation. "We should call Clay."

"Simon, if we aren't back in twenty minutes, call the sheriff and let him know what we're doing. I know right now he has his hands full. I want to make sure there's a reason for him to come."

He crossed to the back exit from the garage and went through it first, scanning the terrain around him. There was still a faint light in the sky, but dusk would soon totally disappear. "Bella, heel and guard Sadie." He didn't want his dog to leave Sadie's side even if Bella sensed danger.

A path cut through the woods from the rear of his yard to Katie's. He wanted to use the cover of the trees as he scouted out whatever Sadie thought she saw. It could be a neighbor heading home after a hike, an animal, the intruders, or a figment of her imagination.

He stopped halfway across the back of Katie's property, planting himself behind a large pine tree. With Sadie and Bella behind him, Brock lifted the binoculars as a bank of clouds obscured the faint light remaining. He slowly swept the panorama of the backyard from the right. The tense set of his shoulders ached.

Sadie gripped his arm. "I see something on the left side of the house."

FIVE

As Brock swung his binoculars to the left, a clanging sound echoed through the air. The noise sent relief through him. "I think it's a bear. Katie's garbage can is on that side behind a cage. A bear could be trying to get into it."

"Are you sure?"

"Stay here. I'll confirm it." Brock moved through the woods until he had a view of the bear lumbering away after being foiled in getting any food. Brock hurried back. "It's a black bear I've seen around here from time to time. That's why when I go hiking, I take a gun and bear spray. So far, I haven't needed to use them. Usually when I see fresh evidence of a bear or a big cat that's moved through the area, I go in the opposite direction."

"Can we stay a few minutes longer to make sure it isn't the two thugs coming back? Are we safe from the bear?"

"Probably. I'm hungry, but we'll stay ten minutes if you'll rest tonight—not sitting at the window in the dining room."

She glanced at the area where the bear had been. "No, I can't sleep. The thugs will likely return later when it's totally dark and most people are asleep."

"I'll take turns with you. Will that satisfy you?"

"Yes."

The sound of that one word made him wonder if she'd smiled. It was too dark to tell. As they headed back to his place, they walked side by side with Bella between them.

"How long did you say you had Bella?"

"Nearly three years. At first, I didn't think there was anything she could do for me. She proved me wrong within a couple of months. I'm so glad I was wrong. And now Bella and I've worked to save hikers who get lost around here. I've enjoyed that and so does Bella. She's getting better and better at tracking."

"I can see why you like doing that. You became a Marine to help people in need."

"I forgot that for a few years. Bella's the one who showed me I could make a difference in others' lives. I used to deny I could hike in rugged country because of my artificial leg. Then a little boy went missing, and they needed a lot of volunteers. I learned I could manage fine. I just needed the right kind of prosthetic leg." Talking about his leg with people hadn't been easy for several years, but now he didn't mind.

As they entered the kitchen from the garage, Simon turned on the burner with the pan of oil on it. "I was just about to call the sheriff. I don't know about you two, but I'm starving. Dinner will be ready soon whether you're here or not. Was there anyone at Katie's?"

"Yes, a bear trying to get into her garbage cans. When he couldn't, he left." Brock followed Sadie into the dining room.

She immediately went back to her post in front of the window that gave her the best view of her sister's place. "I have to admit I'm starving, too."

"We never had lunch." He pulled up a chair and sat near her. "How do you want to handle tonight? I can watch first or get some sleep and take the second shift. Or the other way around. Whatever works best for you."

"I don't think I could sleep anytime soon, so I'll take the first watch. I know you think it's a waste of time. You don't have to do it."

"First, it's not a waste of time. I don't believe Katie will come back, but the two intruders may try."

"Why don't you think Katie will come home?"

"Her supervisor was murdered. Whatever's going down, Katie's somehow caught up in it because the people who killed Tom Connors came after her."

Sadie's eyes grew round. "I wish I'd been wrong about her being in danger, but you're right. She's involved, and she probably has an idea of what's going on. She called me upset. It likely has something to do with where she works. She never talked much about her work. What do they do?"

"They're a global shipping company. They have ties all over the world. They're expanding and growing fast. This could have something to do with them. Tomorrow, we'll go back over to her house and see if there's anything there to indicate what's going on. Maybe we'll find a clue that will point us in the right direction."

"What if Katie witnessed Tom's murder and fled?"

"Does she usually go to her supervisor's house on her day off?"

"I don't know. I haven't been back long, but I should know this stuff. In the past, we knew everything about each other, but then I moved away."

"Because of me?"

She nodded. "When you came back here, I couldn't stay."

Her voice wavered at the end, and the urge to draw her into his arms swamped him. It would only make the situation even more strained. Still, he wouldn't leave her until they found Katie. That was the least he could do. "I'll keep in touch with Clay. Maybe we'll get a break and discover she's safe somewhere. Can you think of anywhere she might go?"

"Normally I'd say my duplex, but I haven't given her a spare key yet. I was going to get one made."

"What's the address of your new place in Butte City?"

She hesitated, her teeth worrying her bottom lip.

"In case we get separated. I won't show up without an invitation."

"I still haven't unpacked all my boxes. There just hasn't been enough time to do that and keep my podcasts going." Sadie gave him the duplex address on Pine Street.

"Speaking of your podcasts reminds me how much I enjoyed your cooking videos," Simon said from the entrance into the kitchen. "Dinner is served. I got the cooking gene in our family."

Brock laughed. "And he constantly complains that I don't have the right ingredients when he comes to see me. Sadie, I'll fix a plate for you or watch Katie's house while you get your meal."

She stood, stretching. "I'm not very hungry, but it's hard to resist that scent of fried chicken."

Simon grinned. "It's your recipe. It's one of my favorites."

"Thanks." She disappeared into the kitchen while Brock positioned himself in front of the window. Memories of Sadie trying to cook for him inundated him. He'd missed those times when his life had been carefree.

Both Simon and Brock ate in the dining room to keep Sadie company. He let his younger brother dominate the conversation while he focused on the myriad questions surrounding what had happened earlier and Katie's disappearance. When Brock finished his dinner, he hopped up and volunteered to do the dishes. He needed space between Sadie and him. He hadn't been prepared to see her so soon.

After cleaning up, Brock moved a more comfortable chair into the dining room for Sadie. Then he made a bed on his living room couch. He wanted to be near the front entrance in case the two intruders decided to breach his house. He walked toward the kitchen to grab his rifle.

When he returned to the dining room, Sadie swiveled her attention toward him, her gaze latching onto the weapon in his hand. "Expecting trouble tonight?"

"It's a possibility, and I want to be prepared if it happens. I don't usually sleep more than six hours a day. I'll relieve you in three hours. In the meantime, I'll be in the living room. Bella will stay with you."

Sadie bent over and petted his dog. "Thanks. She's been a comfort."

He nodded his head once and left. He relaxed the taut grip he had on his gun. All the emotions he'd spent years suppressing were swirling around in his brain. He wasn't the same person Sadie had fallen in love with, but she still was. That gave him a huge barrier to overcome.

Brock lay on the couch while his brother

went to the spare bedroom. Brock looked around, catching a glimpse of Bella and Sadie's left hand on the arm of the chair. With a long sigh, he settled his head on the pillow, staring at the ceiling until his eyelids grew heavy and he went to sleep...

While Brock cleared a hut with a dirt floor, an explosion sounded close by. He turned around suddenly to go help if needed, but he stepped on a hidden landmine. As he dove to the side, the bomb detonated, rocking his world. He hit the ground, pain ripping through him, and everything darkened...

Brock bolted up to a sitting position on the couch. Sweat drenched him, running in rivulets down his body. His heart thudded against his ribcage at a rapid rate. He automatically reached for Bella who always slept next to him. She wasn't there, and for a few seconds, panic gripped him.

As his gaze swept his surroundings, reality slowly took hold. He was in his house in Colorado. The soft light from the kitchen illuminated Bella next to the chair Sadie sat in, but his dog was turned toward him, staring at him.

"Come, Bella," he whispered.

His golden retriever covered the distance between them in a few seconds. He hugged her. The rapid beat of his heart slowed. The knot in his stomach began to unravel as he held Bella.

It had been six months since his last nightmare about what happened to him. He'd thought he'd finally dealt with his last one. But when he considered what had happened today, he shouldn't be surprised.

He released a long breath and rubbed his cheek against Bella. The tension siphoned from him quicker than usual. He shoved to his feet and decided to take Sadie's place early.

When he entered the dining room, he said in a soft voice, not wanting to surprise her, "I'll watch Katie's house now. Go to bed."

No response.

He quickened his steps, and from what little light from the kitchen indicated, she'd fallen asleep in the chair. He shook her arm gently, hating to wake her. She needed the sleep but in a more comfortable place.

Her eyes popped open, and she sat straight up. "It's been three hours already?"

"No, only two. I had a nightmare. I'm not going back to sleep. You need yours. Use my bedroom."

"Yours?"

"I don't have a bed in the third room upstairs. I use that as an office. I'm a financial planner. Simon's in the second one."

"You also need more than two hours sleep." Sadie rose too fast and wobbled.

He reached out to her at the same time she did to him. They embraced each other. Instead of releasing their grasp, they both froze—only inches apart. He wanted to pull her to him, hold her, shield her, and reassure her they would find out what was going on with her sister.

Against all he wanted to do, he finally backed away to allow her to leave. "Go to bed. I can't sleep after I have a nightmare."

She hesitated for a moment. She

opened her mouth as though she wanted to tell him something, but instead, she closed it and hurried from the room with Bella following her.

Brock turned toward the window and stared into the darkness. Now that it was after midnight, he decided to move outside with his night vision binoculars and his rifle. Earlier, he had placated Sadie by letting her watch from the window because he didn't want her to go with him. He didn't want her in danger. There was a crop of rocks on this side of Katie's house that would give him a better vantage point to watch the place from the front and back as well as keep an eye on his home, too.

He hunkered down between the boulders and lifted his binoculars to assess the situation. Occasionally, a set of headlights would pierce the darkness as a car went by on the highway, but no vehicles turned onto the paved driveway to Katie's.

As the hours passed, Brock fought to keep back memories of the times he had to scout and surveil the enemy. Was that why he had the nightmare earlier? He didn't want to relive those moments—especially now that he was putting his life back together. But the hours prior to dawn were his enemy. He went through that day he was shot and couldn't see a way he could have changed the outcome. If only—his life would be much different today.

* * *

Sadie's eyes shot open, her heart racing as a surge of panic swept through her. For a few seconds she couldn't remember where she was. Then she did—in Brock's bed with Bella next to her. He had invaded her dream. She twisted toward the nightstand to see the time. Six o'clock in the morning. She needed to get away at least for a while.

When she'd first lay down, she hadn't thought she would be able to sleep, especially with the constant reminders around her of that day in Brock's hospital room when he told her he didn't want to marry her. At first, she'd assumed he'd meant they would have to postpone the wedding until he was better, but he quickly made it clear he didn't want to marry her— ever. She hadn't thought he would say that. Their connection had been so strong. She'd supported his desire to serve in the U.S. Marines. His grandfather had been a general in the same branch of service, and when he died from cancer, Brock had wanted to follow in his granddad's military footsteps.

If only he hadn't been wounded. If only he'd believed in her to be there for him.

She swung her legs over the side of the bed and stood. She needed to get out of here. Being near Brock like this was tearing her up inside.

Bella hopped down and sat near her, laying her head in Sadie's lap. She rubbed the dog and bent over to kiss the top of the golden retriever's head. "I can see why you're so special to Brock."

As she slipped her shoes on, a thought inundated her. What if Katie had been trying to call her on her cell phone or at her house? She needed to go check then get back into Katie's house to see if there was a message that she hadn't seen with all the destruction in the living room. The sight of it had shocked her. As children, she and Katie had a secret code they'd used all the time. One could have been left at either one of the houses. Had Katie left her a message somewhere? She hoped so, because she couldn't get rid of the feeling her sister was in serious trouble.

Intending to tell Brock of her plan, she grabbed her jacket and hurried down the stairs with Bella at her side. When she entered the dining room, the chair was empty. She checked the lower floor. Where was he?

"Find Brock," she said to his dog.

Bella headed into the kitchen and planted herself in front of the door to the garage. Sadie opened it and noted both her and Brock's cars were there as well as Simon's motorcycle. So where had Brock gone? As she turned back into the room, she noticed that his rifle was gone. She walked to the window where she'd watched Katie's house. As the sky began to lighten, she spied Brock in a cluster of rocks where they used to play as children. At least, he was all right and that location was a good one, but she wished he'd told her. For a few minutes, she'd thought he was in danger like her sister.

This was the perfect time for her to leave and go to her home in Butte City to see if Katie had tried to contact her again. Brock was keeping an eye on her family home. She could go and return in an hour. She would have the foresight to leave him a note, letting him know her plans— something he should have done earlier. She grabbed a pen and paper, scribbled an explanation, then left it where he'd be sure to see it.

She'd only moved here a few days ago. The likelihood the intruders yesterday knew where she lived was slim.

She exited to the garage, leaving Bella behind. As the door rose, she hurried around her car and hopped into the driver's seat, stuffing her purse in her glove box. Quickly, she backed out and drove to the highway. Then she turned on her headlights. As much as Brock was trying to help her, she needed a break. Being around him brought up all the turmoil she'd gone through four years ago.

She started to pull over at the cell reception parking lot to wait for her messages to download but decided not to. By then, any emails or texts would be on her phone. Chances were that Brock would come after her. She'd told him her address. She didn't want a confrontation with him right now because the past twenty hours had played havoc with her nerves, so she would hurry and be on her way back to his house before he was aware she was gone.

Dawn brightened as she pulled into her garage. Everything looked normal.

Katie had wanted her to stay with her and rent an office for her work in Butte City, but when she'd discovered Brock lived next door in his family's home, she'd said no. She'd been right to say that because what she feared had happened. Her anger at Brock and her love for him tangled together in her stomach, leaving a hard knot. She'd thought she was over him—or at least she'd convinced herself she was—but so many conflicting feelings bombarded her. She couldn't forget how close they had been at one time.

Before leaving her car, she picked up her cell phone to see what messages she had. She ignored all the business-related ones and zeroed in on two from her sister.

The first one said, "Just in case you left already, turn around. Don't come. I'm leaving. I saw Tom being murdered."

Katie had witnessed her supervisor being killed. Had she seen who did it? Was it the two thugs who broke into her house?

She quickly read the next one only seconds after the first voicemail message was sent. "Stay away. There's so much I want to tell you, but I don't have the time. I wish instead this was like one of the games we loved to play when we were kids. Love you."

And I love you, Katie. I'm going to find you.

She slid from her front seat and stuffed her cell phone into her pocket in case Katie contacted her again while she was here.

After entering her place, she crossed to her landline phone that she mainly used for radio appearances and saw there was a message.

When she played it, she was disappointed that it was Katie's first voicemail. Nothing new that would help her to figure out the location of her twin sister. What if those intruders finally found her? She deleted the message.

She went into her bedroom and grabbed a duffel bag. As much as she wanted to stay here, she needed to be up on the mountain looking for her sister. At least now she knew why Katie had fled. Once the thugs were caught, Katie could come out of hiding.

Sadie dressed in clothes that were better for hiking the area around the family home. The second message gave her a direction to look for her sister.

Like one of the games we loved to play when we were kids.

There were a few places they'd loved to go—like a secret club. Katie's words gave her hope this would end soon.

After packing, Sadie picked up her duffel bag, left her bedroom, and started for the garage. She stopped. Just in case Brock didn't find her note at his place, she picked up a pen on the table where her landline phone sat to jot down a quick note she was heading back to his house.

A sound at her door caught her attention. Was someone trying to get into her place through the front door, as if the person was picking her lock? Was it Brock? She hurried to a window and peeked out, glimpsing an unfamiliar car parked in front of her duplex.

SIX

The sound of Brock's garage door raising interrupted the dawn's quiet. He swiveled around and saw Sadie's car driving fast toward the highway. In the semi-darkness he couldn't tell who was driving or how many people might be inside the vehicle. Had something happened at his house?

He shot up from between the boulders and ran toward his garage where the door was still up. His rifle gripped in his hands, he entered his home through the kitchen, having no idea what he would find. As he made his way through the rooms, he berated himself for leaving. What if the thugs figured out that Sadie was at his place? At least the first floor appeared all right.

He ran up the stairs and into the opened doorway of his bedroom, flipping on the overhead light. Bella lay on the bed and perked up when he came toward her. She jumped down and followed him.

"This is when I wish you could talk." Brock also wished he could have seen who was inside her car. He moved toward the connected bathroom and peered inside. No Sadie.

He returned to the hallway, checked his office, then the second bedroom. His brother lay sprawled across the coverlet in the clothes he had worn all day. Brock turned the switch on the wall and bright light wiped away all the darkness.

Simon groaned and pulled the pillow over his head. "Go away. It's too early."

"Sadie's gone."

His brother struggled to sit up, his forehead scrunched up. "Gone? Where?"

"I don't know. Did the phone ring?"

"I didn't hear anything."

He wasn't even sure Simon would have heard a loud noise, but Brock had to ask him. If no one had broken into his home, then why had Sadie left? Where would she go? "Get up. You need to watch this place and Katie's while I try and find Sadie. If something doesn't feel right, call the sheriff and then me."

"Where are you going?"

"I'm going to check Sadie's duplex. Thankfully, last night she gave me her address in Butte City. That's the only place I can think she would go to right now."

Simon rolled to a standing position, his shoulder length, dark brown hair a mess. He finger-combed it. "What if Sadie calls here? What do I tell her?"

"Find out where she is and tell her to stay put. Then if she's some place besides her house, let me know." As he walked into the hallway, Brock added, "I have a shotgun where I keep my rifle. Keep it with you in case you're confronted by someone, but don't put yourself in a bad situation if the intruders return. Call Clay first. Then me."

Simon followed Brock. "I will. Why would Sadie leave by herself?"

Brock kept walking toward the garage. "Most likely Sadie thinks that Katie might have contacted her again before she fled the house. She wouldn't know unless she could get her text messages on her cell phone. Sadie can get impatient and act without thinking the situation through. I should have realized she might attempt it. Her connection with Katie is extremely strong. Rational thought can go out the window when it involves her twin." Sadie had always been the risk taker while Katie hadn't been.

When he left his house, he pushed the speed limit as much as he could on the curvy highway down the mountain. He hoped that she'd stopped at the cell-reception parking lot and waited there until the texts finally downloaded to her cell phone, which might take some time depending on her phone provider and how many texts she had. And it was always possible that Katie hadn't sent a text to Sadie.

He slowed as he took the last curve, but when he saw no cars at the parking lot for cell reception, he continued toward Butte City and Sadie's duplex, praying she was there and all right.

* * *

Sadie looked around frantically for a way to escape or a weapon to use. The patio door caught her attention. She hurried to it and unlocked it. As she ran into her backyard, someone breached her front entrance. She glimpsed a tall thin man in a black ski mask and turned her focus on finding a way to escape the assailant. Her gaze fixed on the rear chain-link fence. If she could get over it...

From her left a blur of black rammed into her. She hit the ground, a thug pinning her down with his heavy, stocky body. Blue eyes—chilling eyes—stared at her from behind a black ski mask. It had to be the same man who fired at Brock and her from the garage yesterday. But she didn't have any kind of weapon to use on him like she had his partner in Katie's bedroom. Instead, she would use the pen still in her hand to poke his eyes out. But he grasped each wrist and pinned her arms above her head so fast she hadn't been able to execute her plan.

Sadie screamed, "Help. I'm being attacked," praying a neighbor was home and could hear her.

He gripped both of her wrists with one hand. The pen she still held dropped to the ground as her assailant hit her in the jaw.

When his fist connected with her face again, pain streaked outward from the contact. She had to think of something else to do, but it was hard to put together thoughts in her swirling mind.

He flipped her over and tied her hands behind her back. Her left cheek, that he'd struck, was pressed into the grass, intensifying the agony. Her thoughts spun faster and faster. The feel of a prick on her neck sent her falling into a black void.

* * *

Brock's call to Sadie's cell phone went to voicemail. Alarm bells clanged in his head. The urgency to get to her as fast as he could swamped him, and he pressed his foot on the accelerator. When he arrived at her duplex, her car wasn't parked in the driveway. He hoped it was in her garage.

He ran toward the front entrance and tried the knob. It turned. His gut knotted. Sadie wouldn't have left her house open. He took out his cell phone as he entered her place and called Clay.

"I'm at Sadie's duplex, and the place isn't locked up. Something's happened here."

"I'm on my way. I'll contact the chief of police. What's the address?"

"Sadie's rear door is ajar." He told the sheriff where she lived. "Hurry."

Brock stuffed his phone back into his

pocket and headed toward the kitchen to see if her car was parked in the garage. When it was, he gripped the rifle he'd brought with him until his fingers ached. He couldn't wait for Clay. He needed to search the whole duplex to see if she...

Emotions he usually kept buried jammed his throat. She had to be alive.

Lord, please protect her. I've seen so much death. I don't know how I could handle hers.

He went from room to room, making his way around the stacked boxes she hadn't emptied yet. A few were knocked over, and the items in it searched. He returned to the living room and headed out the back door, making sure not to mess up any potential fingerprints. He crossed the small patio and scanned the area. Had she run away? Where would she go? His gaze latched onto the chain-link fence running along the rear of the property. The sides of the yard had a six-foot wooden fence—harder to climb. As he started for the back, he spied a pen on the ground. From its new condition, it had to be recently placed there. He looked closer and found fresh drops of blood nearby. The knot in his gut solidified as he straightened.

He spied Clay at the rear exit and motioned for him to come. "I think this is where Sadie was taken down."

With gloves on, Clay took a photo of the area then picked up the pen and dropped it into an evidence bag. "I'm calling for two deputies to gather evidence. I'll have the fingerprints on the pen checked against Sadie's in the house."

Brock looked up at the early morning sky. "Maybe a neighbor saw something. A car out front possibly. Sadie's is in the garage."

When the deputies showed up, Brock and Clay went house to house. No one answered the door at the other half of the duplex.

Brock stepped off the porch and glanced in the front window. The living room was bare. "I don't think anyone lives here."

Clay joined him and sighed. "I'd hoped

someone did and might have heard something."

Most of the people on the block were home and hadn't left for work yet, but no one could tell them anything.

Finally, the person who lived across the street from Sadie had a surveillance camera that might have footage to help them. Then another older couple a few houses down had gone for their early morning walk and had noticed a car outside the duplex.

The white-haired woman invited them inside while she called her husband to join them. "I'm Esther Dodd. I haven't seen that car before We're part of the neighborhood watch, so both Bud and I keep an eye on what's going on around here."

"What color and make was the car?" Clay asked as Bud came from the back.

"It was a gray car with dark windows. Hard to see inside." Esther smiled at her husband. "I don't know the make, but I'm sure Bud does."

"It was an older Honda Accord, in good condition—at least it looked that way to me," the older man answered. "I was going to get the license plate number on the way home if it was still there. But it wasn't. We go down several blocks then over two then circle back. I thought it could be a new tenant for the vacant duplex, and we were going to welcome them to the neighborhood."

Clay thanked them and turned to leave.

Brock shook their hands. "Thank you." He paused. "The lady across the street from the duplex has a surveillance camera. Do you know anyone else on this block who has one?"

"Not many. That's why Esther and I go walking a lot. All I have is a camera doorbell, but it doesn't work. I'm definitely getting it replaced right now."

"Bud, remember the neighbor next to the duplex on the right has a camera." Esther took a couple of steps to the edge of her porch and pointed to the house next to Sadie's. "They may have already left for work. Both are school teachers."

"Thanks, again." Brock joined Clay on the sidewalk. "Our best shot is Sadie's neighbor to the right, according to Esther."

They crossed the street and rang the bell. Not seconds after that the garage door went up. Brock stayed on the porch while Clay stepped into the driveway. When the young couple greeted the sheriff, Brock came to his friend's side. The wife looked as if she was going to work while the man didn't.

The wife's eyes grew wide when she looked next door at several cars from the sheriff department. "Is something wrong?" Her voice quavered.

The sheriff stepped forward. "We're asking people on this street if they have any outside surveillance cameras. The couple across the street said you did."

Her husband nodded. "I'm Sam Baldwin and this is my wife, Sue. We do."

"Can you get us the video for the past ninety minutes?" Clay asked. "It's important."

"Yes, it's on my cell phone. I'll go get it." Sam left them and went back inside.

Sue's face went pale. "Did something happen to Sadie? She just moved in."

Brock glanced at her. "You know Sadie?"

"Yes, we went to church together when she lived here." She tilted her head. "You look familiar."

Brock didn't go to Sadie's church. "I'm a friend of hers. Maybe you remember me from Butte City High School."

She snapped her fingers. "That's it. You two dated."

"Yes. Did you see or hear anything unusual in the last hour?"

She stared at the ground for a moment. When she lifted her head and looked at Brock, she said, "No, I'm sorry. I listen to the radio when I get up."

When her husband returned with his phone, Clay gave him the email address to send it to him. "If either one of you remember anything unusual around dawn or hear something from one of your neighbors about this morning, please give me a call."

"We will. I'm a big fan of Sadie's. Her recipes are great. I was excited when I saw her move in next door." Sue shook her head. "I can't believe something might have happened to her. I sure hope not."

Me, too. Brock had forgotten how determined Sadie could be. The bond between her and Katie was strong, and he should have anticipated Sadie would go to any extreme to find her sister. "Thank you for your help."

As Brock returned to Sadie's duplex, the same guilt hit him that he'd felt about his last skirmish in the Middle East, leaving him and others hurt or dead. He should have been able to prevent the losses somehow. What if he never saw Sadie again?

SEVEN

The pain that hammered against Sadie's skull drew her unwillingly to consciousness. The scent of blood on her lips and the pulsating agony slowly brought her totally awake. She raised her head and opened her eyes to pitch-black surroundings. She tried to move, but she was tied to a hardback chair.

How did she...? Words evaded her. She tried to remember. The last thing she recalled was running out of her house. What happened?

Where am I?

She tried to scour her mind, but it was a dark wasteland. All she could focus on was the intensifying ache on the left side of her face. She ran her tongue over her dried lips and tasted blood—metallic, nauseating. Her stomach roiled.

Her eyelids slid closed. Keeping them open in the dark took too much effort.

* * *

Brock paced Clay's office as he brought up the surveillance footage from Sadie's two neighbors. Not a lot to go on. "Let's look at Sam and Sue's first."

"That's what I thought, too, and then the one across the street." Clay punched a button and the first video came up.

Brock stood behind Clay's chair and watched over his friend's shoulder.

Not long after Sadie drove into her garage, a gray Honda Accord pulled up to the duplex. One man, dressed in black and wearing a ski mask, hurried toward Sadie's front door while another headed for the backyard. They disappeared from the camera's view before they reached the porch and the side yard. Brock squeezed both hands into fists, trying to calm his escalating rage.

Clay fast-forwarded the footage until the tall, thin man came back out front and waved to the driver in the Honda to move it to Sadie's driveway. The driver, a man of about six feet and average build, exited the car and surveyed the street. A few seconds later, two men—one tall and thin, the other short and husky—rushed from the duplex carrying something large covered in a sheet.

Clay paused the tape. "That's got to be Sadie." He pressed the key to restart the recording again.

The tall guy slid into the backseat with what was wrapped in a sheet while the stocky man climbed into the front passenger seat. Then the driver quickly left. Gone in seconds. Was Sadie alive? "What about the handgun Sadie took from one of the intruders yesterday? Anything from it?

"No fingerprints but Sadie's. However, it matched the weapon used to kill Connors. The gun was reported stolen months ago. I checked the whereabouts of the owner who had reported it stolen. He's on a business trip to England. Speaking about fingerprints, Sadie's were the only ones on the pen."

In the second footage from across the street where the driver pulled into the driveway, the license plate number was visible. Brock started pacing again while Clay ran the license plate and wrote down the address of the owner. "I'll put a BOLO out on the car. Be right back."

While Clay left his office, Brock called Simon. "Anything happen?"

"Nothing. I told you I would call."

"I think the same two thugs who ransacked Katie's house also took Sadie from her duplex with a third assailant."

"Is she alive?"

"We don't know yet." The picture of the two kidnappers carrying out what had to be Sadie flooded Brock's mind with all the emotions he'd tried to keep at bay—rage at the helplessness inundating him, fear he would never see her again, and determination to protect her. He needed to remain calm and focused in order to get her back—alive. If they had wanted her dead, they would have left her at her house. No, for some reason the kidnappers thought she could help them. "I wanted to let you know we have the license plate and description of the car." Brock gave Simon the information. "That's just in case they come back up the mountain. Let me know. Do not confront them."

"I will, and I won't approach them. I'm upstairs in your office. I have a good view of the front of the two houses as well as the area between them."

"Good. I'll keep you informed of what's going on." Brock disconnected from the call as the door to Clay's office opened and he came into the room. "Whose car is it?"

"An elderly couple, the Bensons, reported it stolen this morning when they woke up. My deputies, as well as the state police and other law enforcement agencies in the surrounding counties, are looking for the car."

"So what can I do? I've got to do something."

"You can review traffic cams in Butte City and see if you can spot the car. The more people looking at the tapes the faster we'll find out which way they went."

"You think the kidnappers took her out of Butte City?" Brock prowled the office, needing to keep moving.

"Not necessarily. They could be still in town."

He'd never paid attention to where the traffic cams were posted. "Are there ways out of the city without being caught on tape?"

"Yes. I realize looking at the footage might not produce anything, but we still need to rule it out. Most of my deputies are out driving around, which leaves only one to go through the tapes."

"Where do I go to do this?"

"Deputy Olson's in the first interview room. He's setting it up now. I hope we can catch the car right after the kidnapping. It'll give us the direction they went."

Brock stopped at the door. "If you hear anything, please let me know."

"I will."

Brock left the sheriff's office and walked down the hallway to the interview room. He hated feeling helpless, hated thinking of Sadie in danger—maybe hurt—so having some way to search for her helped to keep him focused and calm.

An hour later when he and Deputy Olson ran out of footage to review, Brock stood and paced, disappointed there wasn't one sighting of the car after taking Sadie—as though they knew where the traffic cams were. "Do you have a detailed map of the town I could use?"

The deputy nodded and rose. "I'll be right back."

When Olson returned, he marked every area that had a traffic cam. Then they both noted the areas where they'd reviewed the footage.

While the deputy left to get Clay, Brock stood back and studied the map until the sheriff entered with Olson.

"There are three ways the kidnappers could have avoided a traffic cam and leave Butte City after taking Sadie." Brock pointed to the streets, drawing with his finger how the kidnappers could take her out of town, giving them more places to hide her, without ever showing up on a traffic cam. "If I was one of them, I would go up into the mountains. The first leads up into the mountain east of the town and the second one to the mountain on the west side. This third way leads to a main highway."

Clay tilted his head and assessed the diagram. "I'll let the state police know about these routes. We'll put more manpower on those three possibilities."

Brock took a pencil and made a circle on the northwest part of Butte City. "What if the two men changed cars?"

"They might. Hopefully, if they steal another car, which seems to be their mode operandi, we'll know and can see where they went from that location. We were able to track part of the kidnappers' trip from the Bensons to the victim's duplex," Deputy Olson said.

When the deputy said victim, Brock ground his teeth, set his fisted hands on the table, then leaned over the map—there was so much area to search. "I'm not sure we narrowed down the options of where she might be. These kidnappers probably killed Tom Connors. Two of them fit the description we have so far." He didn't want to think about what they could do to Sadie.

Clay tapped one area. "I'm going to have several deputies concentrate here near the west side of town. There's a large park in the middle that needs to be checked. Too bad the car didn't have GPS. That would have been a big help. If we find the stolen vehicle abandoned, then we know we're going to need more people for a search and possibly change tactics. They did that when they stole Tom Connors' SUV and went to Katie's house."

It felt like Brock was back overseas in the middle of a war and trying to figure out where their enemy was. That day when his unit found the village where their foe had been, the massacres of the villagers consumed his focus until he stepped on a booby trap, hidden beneath the ground. Several others in his unit didn't survive their encounter with a landmine. He'd been told later that he'd been lucky, but he hadn't felt that way.

"If we're going to check the park, I'm going to bring Bella to help track Sadie's scent."

"Good. Bring something our other dogs can use to track Sadie." Clay rolled up the map and headed for the door. "Deputy Olson, you stay here to man the phones. Brock, I'll meet you at Black Bear Park."

When he'd left his home earlier, he should have brought Bella with him, but he didn't want his brother left alone in case the intruders returned to Katie's place. Simon could handle a shotgun, but not much more. His little brother preferred living in a big city like Denver.

* * *

Besides the darkness surrounding Sadie, the silence, and having no idea what the time was caused her heart to race and her breaths to come out in short puffs. Lightheadedness attacked her. It seemed like the blackness swirled before her, although she couldn't really see anything spinning in the darkness. Nausea roiled in her stomach.

But slowly, whatever the kidnapper gave her was wearing off.

She wouldn't give up. She tested the ropes that bound her wrists together behind her and her ankles to the chair legs. All she succeeded in doing was rubbing her skin raw. Next she tried to move the hardback chair she sat in. When she did, the sound reverberated through the quiet. She stopped and listened.

A door to the right banged open and bright light flooded a small part of the room, giving her a glimpse of where she was. The wooden floor looked old and worn. The wall where the tall man stood was painted a light color, but on closer inspection it was peeling in strips.

The kidnapper slammed the door closed with him inside. Darkness returned until he shined a bright light on her. She shifted her gaze from one side to the other and spied a window—at least what she thought was one with a shade over it. On its right side, a faint streak of light invaded the room, but not really strong enough to give her an idea where she was or what the surroundings were like.

Her abductor moved closer. She smelled cigarette smoke, but, otherwise, she could tell little about him.

"Katie, where's the flash drive?"

"What flash drive?" Good. He thought she was Katie. At least that meant they wouldn't be looking for her twin now.

"The one you stole from Mason and Fox."

Why would her twin do that? She was one of the most honest people Sadie knew.

He decreased the space between them, the brightness of the light nearly blinding her. "If you tell me, this will go much easier for you."

Yeah, sure. "I gave it to Tom Connors, my supervisor." She had no idea if her sister had done that, but the guy was dead, and this kidnapper and his partner were the ones who probably murdered him.

He slapped her face on the side his partner had hit her before. "He didn't have it."

The pain of the blow stung her cheek. The room really did seem to swirl before her eyes. This time, she glimpsed his arm going back to strike her again, and she quickly said, "It's at my house."

"We looked."

"Obviously not hard enough."

Instead of hitting her, he grabbed her shirt in his hand and leaned over until he was inches from her face. "We didn't have time. No more stall tactics. Where is it? Your life depends on your answer."

She was sure he could hear her heart beating. Its sound filled her ears, and if he hadn't been so close, she wouldn't have heard his threat. "I can show you."

"No. The police were all over your place."

"The flash drive isn't hidden in the cabin. It's at the duplex."

He gathered more of her shirt and pushed his fist into her throat until he nearly choked her. "Don't play games with me. I was told you lived at the mountain cabin. Where is it?" He was in her face, the stench of cigarette smoke nauseating her.

"I—can't," barely squeaked out of her mouth.

He loosened his hold slightly.

She gulped in a large breath of air. "I bought the duplex as an investment and a place I could stay occasionally, especially in the winter when the snow can make the roads impassable."

"It's in one of those boxes?"

"Yes."

"Which one?" His gruff voice indicated the end of his patience.

"It's the bottom box I put in the closet of the first bedroom. At least I think. I had two movers, and that's where I told them to put the box it's in. I can come with you and point it out."She realized she was digging herself into a hole, but hopefully, by now, Brock knew where she went when she left his place. She had no idea how much time had passed since her arrival at her duplex. If she went with the kidnappers, then she would try to get away. If they left her here, she would do the same. At least she knew where a window was.

"You better be telling me the truth. I can make your life miserable and painful." He released his grip on her shirt and checked the ropes around her wrists, chest, and ankles. She inflated her lungs with air before he yanked each restraint to make sure they were tight.

She gritted her teeth. She didn't want to give him the satisfaction of knowing he'd hurt her more.

When he left, Sadie released a long breath that had given her some wiggle room with the rope around her chest. She sank back against the hard-wooden slats and listened for any indication the kidnapper was gone. The sound of a door closing somewhere in the place finally resonated through the quiet. Where was the stocky guy? Did they both leave? She had to risk that she was alone. For a few minutes, she waited to make sure her abductor didn't return.

With her feet flat on the wooden floor, she crouched over and put her weight totally down on them. She could move each one a couple of inches, slowly scooting the chair toward the window. When she crashed into a table, she held her breath, hoping nothing toppled to the floor. When it didn't, she maneuvered around the table, praying nothing else was between her and the window. She used her head to work her way between the blackout shade and the wall. Daylight streamed through the gap, blinding her for a moment. Blinking repeatedly helped her get accustomed to the brightness.

A forest surrounded her, but it was daunting that she wasn't on the first floor. The drop to the ground had to be twelve to fourteen feet. She was trapped.

EIGHT

Brock stared at the stolen car found in the park in an area with dense vegetation. The rear of the vehicle sticking out of thick brush caught a deputy sheriff's attention as law enforcement officers scoured the five-hundred-acre woodlands with hiking trails. Brock stood back, holding Bella's leash while Clay and a deputy thoroughly checked the sedan.

Clay motioned to Brock. "Bring Bella."

He let his golden retriever smell Sadie's jacket then handed it to a nearby officer who took it to another handler with his dog. "Find Sadie." Brock headed to the sheriff.

Bella went to the sedan, stopped at the

backseat, hopped in, and barked.

Again Brock gave her the command to keep looking for Sadie. His dog left the car on the other side. "Stay." Brock had dropped her leash rather than crawl through the vehicle, like Bella had done. He didn't want to disturb the evidence gathered from the scene.

Brock picked up the leash and said again, "Find Sadie."

Bella took off into the trees, pausing and sniffing the air every once in a while. Clay followed them. She came to a halt at a dirt-packed parking lot at the edge of the Black Bear Park for people who might hike up the mountain nearby. The trail had evaporated.

Frustrated, Brock raked his fingers through his black hair. "You think she was put into another car?"

"Probably. Have Bella go over the whole parking lot then the perimeter just to make sure."

Brock did, and Bella kept coming back to the same place. "And we have no idea what that car looks like."

"Not unless someone saw a vehicle leave here or reports one stolen soon. At least it would give us something to check. Up the mountain or back into the town." Clay gestured at the tire tracks in the dirt. "This is the only thing we have." He took pictures of them then called for a deputy to make a cast of the tracks. "We'll even do the footprints around this area, but that might be a long shot."

"I think they went up this mountain." Where Brock lived was on a mountain on the other side of Butte City. "Maybe we should visit each cabin."

"I agree. We can put up a road block and check each car that leaves. This is the only road up to the top of the mountain and down it."

Brock started across the parking lot. "Let's go."

"Give me a minute. I know you're impatient to get started, but I need to set up the road block and get more searchers here than just you and me. There are a couple of other SAR dogs we're using in the park, and we need to get them over here and smell the jacket." Clay walked back to his patrol car to contact his second-in-command about what was necessary for a mountain search for Sadie.

Brock stood back, remembering not only the searches he had been involved in since returning to Colorado with Bella, but also the ones he took part in Afghanistan. He tried to focus on the successful ones, but the battle to stay positive that they would find Sadie was hard to maintain since he couldn't forget the ones where he didn't find the victim in time.

Live in the moment. I can't change the past. He repeated those words over and over, and a calmness descended. Brock turned to find Clay still on his phone.

"Contact me if you need me. Brock and I are starting on the right side of the road at the bottom. Have the searchers meet where the no cell reception sign is. Keep me informed on any developments. Also get me the list of any recently stolen vehicles in case we find one." After he hung up, Clay slipped behind his steering wheel. "Since they've stolen three cars that we know of, they might be driving another one."

"I hope so. It would make things easier for us." Brock hurried to his car and followed Clay's patrol car as other law enforcement officers came to join the growing search party.

Brock had been keeping his brother informed when he could. Before he lost his cell reception, he called Simon to see if anything had happened at Katie's house or his.

"It's been quiet. Have you found her?" Simon asked.

"No, but we searched Black Bear Park and found the car that had been seen at Sadie's duplex. It was abandoned. We're searching the southwest side of Black Bear Mountain now. Bella followed her scent, and it appears that they changed cars again. We're hoping she's somewhere on the mountain. I'll be out of cell reception soon. I'll call when I have it again. If anything happens, phone the sheriff's office. They'll be able to get through with the radio. That's how Clay's staying in contact with the rest of the search party."

Brock disconnected and pocketed his cell phone. Half the group went to the top where the road came to an end and were working their way down while Brock set off with Clay up the mountain on the right side of the highway with other searchers spread out. Brock checked his watch. It had been hours since Sadie had been taken. Every minute that passed decreased her chances of being alive when they found her. He would search until he located her.

* * *

Lord, I need Your help. How do I get out of here? What can I do?

Sadie scanned the darkness before her. An idea popped into her mind. There might be a weapon somewhere in this room. Since she'd been able to move herself to the window, she could go to a different place to look for anything that would help her get out of here.

She used her head to manipulate her way between the shade and the window, widening the gap so more light could pour into the room. It was bare of knickknacks and only had a few pieces of furniture—a couch, the end table with a metal lamp but no light bulb, and an overstuffed chair along another wall to the left of the sofa. She could only see the window she was at. There was another door near the one the man used to come into the room. A closet? Maybe there was something inside that would help her get out of here.

But the distance to it seemed yards and yards away. The effects of whatever they gave her still lingered and made her exhausted from her exertion to inch the chair to the window. But she wouldn't let that stop her. She drew in a deep breath.

As she started to maneuver one side forward then the other, another idea came to her. What if she could wiggle the rope down and off the leg of the chair? If that worked, she could do the other one. Then she could try to slide down and work to slip the rope around her chest up, so she could stand. Walking across the room even with her hands still tied would be better and quieter in case the stocky man was still here. She didn't know if it would work, but the one thing she did know was she had to do something to try and get away.

She wedged herself at an angle against the table and the window, lifting one of the front chair legs off the floor while leaning in the opposite direction. She grasped the table with both of her hands that were behind her back. Pulling her limb out as far as the rope would allow—maybe half an inch—she wiggled it slowly down the piece of wood at the same time she had to sink lower in the seat. Her flexibility made it a little easier, but if she didn't get this accomplished soon, she was afraid the man would return when he didn't find the flash drive, and her chance to escape would be gone.

When she managed to free one foot, she set the leg of the chair quietly on the floor. Her weariness had doubled, but she couldn't give up. She took a moment to breathe deeply and rest before working the other foot loose. She wiggled her upper body back up partway, so it was easier to lean the chair to allow her to raise its opposite front leg off the floor.

The sound of a door closing caused her to pause. Her heartbeat increased. Then she heard footsteps coming toward the room she was in.

* * *

Brock stood behind Clay as he knocked on a door to a log cabin set in a grove of trees. A middle-aged woman answered. A little girl clung to the lady's leg. He smiled at the child, and she ducked behind the woman.

"I'm Sheriff Maxwell. Have you seen this young lady in the past day?" He showed her a picture of Sadie that Brock had given to him to use.

"No, but then I haven't left my house today. I'm babysitting my granddaughter."

The little girl peeked around her grandmother and stared at Bella who stood between Brock and the sheriff. The child took a step out from behind her grandmother then another, reaching her arm out to touch his golden retriever.

"Claire, don't touch the strange dog."

The girl, no more than four years old, snatched her arm back and dropped her head forward.

"It's okay with me if your granddaughter pets Bella. She's gentle and loves children."

"Please, Granny." Claire's large gray eyes fixed on his dog reminded him of Sadie's. What if he never saw Sadie again? The thought that could happen stiffened his resolve. He would find her alive one way or another.

"Fine," the older woman said.

Her granddaughter approached Bella cautiously. She lifted her hand and patted

Bella's head for a few seconds then backed away. Brock couldn't help but wonder if they were even looking in the right place. Did the kidnappers think that Sadie was Katie? If they did realize the truth, what would they do to Sadie? She wouldn't be of any use to them. Brock had to shut down the mounting doubts. It never helped him when he searched for a person lost in the mountains or a comrade in a war zone. He'd always managed to overcome those doubts and forge ahead—but this was Sadie, a woman he'd once asked to marry him.

Brock and Bella walked away from the cabin with Clay. "Whose name are you saying is missing?"

Clay stopped. "For now, it's Katie Williams. I'd wanted to keep it as if it was only Katie, but after I found out the next-door neighbor knew it was Sadie because of her cooking podcasts, I realized it would probably come out by the end of the day. I've asked the couple next door to keep it quiet and told the press her identity isn't being revealed because the next of kin hasn't been notified. At the moment, only my officers and the neighbor know about Sadie's disappearance. The search teams and press are using Katie's photo. So far the press doesn't know yet, but that won't last long, especially with the fact Katie's supervisor at work was murdered. It'll be all over the news and probably go national when it breaks."

Which could force the people who took Sadie to kill her and escape. "When the kidnappers realize they don't have Katie, if they don't already know that, they'll probably get rid of Sadie and return to looking for her sister, "Brock said to Clay, hoping his friend could reassure him that wasn't likely.

"That could happen, but we're going to do everything to keep it from occurring."

For a few minutes, Brock felt defenseless like he had when he was in the hospital. He wasn't going to let that feeling of helplessness overwhelm him as it had four years ago. He didn't want to lose a possible second chance with Sadie. Instead, he would turn to the Lord. Sadie and Katie were in His hands.

After checking the area around the cabin, Clay started toward the next residence. "Mr. Taylor lives at the house through the woods." He pointed in that direction.

Brock caught sight of the place, two stories tall and rundown. He unclipped the leash from Bella's collar then took out a piece of the shirt he had with Sadie's scent on it. The other canine teams had taken the jacket and fragments of the shirt he held. He let his dog smell it again then said, "Find Sadie." He did that with each house they approached, and so far, eight places hadn't triggered Bella's response that Sadie was nearby.

His dog sniffed the air and headed into the fir and pine trees between the pieces of property.

Brock picked up his gait. "She's on to something."

As they emerged from the forest, Bella

rushed for the porch to the two-story white house. At the door she sat and barked over and over.

Brock glanced at Clay beside him. "She's here."

As they approached the entrance, Clay called for backup, which was the two deputies across the road. "I'll go around the place to see if there's another way out. Calm Bella down," Clay said to Brock.

When Clay left to circle the place, an old man in his seventies or eighties and hunched over a cane opened the door. "That mutt could wake the dead. I was trying to take a nap. What do you want?" The whole time he spoke, he darted his eyes to the right.

Brock knew fear when he saw it, and this man was afraid. "I'm sorry she woke you up. My dog just took off and ran to your place. Probably saw a squirrel or rabbit. I'll put her on her leash." He leaned over to snap it on the leather collar, but before he could, Bella charged through the gap in the doorway, nearly knocking the elderly man down.

The gentleman had both of his hands on the cane to keep from falling over. Brock reached out to steady the guy.

The front door slammed closed—by someone else.

* * *

The sound of a dog barking overrode all other noise. Sadie quickly leaned the chair back, hoping she could free her other foot before whoever was out in the hallway came into the room. Maybe the noise the animal was making would deter the person who kidnapped her. Maybe it was a search party for her nearing the house. She had to figure out a way to get their attention.

She righted her chair and moved it around, so she could look out the window and let them know where she was. As she stuck her head between the shade and the window, she scanned the area for the sight of anyone. A uniformed man rounded the corner to the front. Clay? All she could do was bang her head against the thick glass. He disappeared from her view.

She sagged against the glass, feeling helpless. She'd missed her chance.

* * *

Brock slammed his shoulder against the door. Out of the corner of his eye, he caught sight of Clay returning to the front. "Bella went inside. Sadie's got to be there."

The sheriff arrived on the porch as two deputies hurried across the yard. He motioned for one to go around the rear then waved Brock back. "Leave this to me and my deputies. Stand aside."

"But Bella and probably Sadie are in there."

"You're a civilian." Clay waited until Brock obeyed then stood next to his deputy and put up one finger, followed by two then three.

They put all their force behind their kicks against the wooden entrance. Their first attempt rattled the door, but it remained shut.

While Clay called for a battering ram, Brock moved toward the side of the house. If he could find which room Sadie was in, that might help. He was afraid that this would turn into a hostage situation with Sadie and Bella in the middle. In the military, he'd been involved in such settings and too many hadn't ended well.

As he headed along the side of the house, he noticed all the shades over the windows were closed on the first floor. He looked up and caught sight of Sadie with her face against the glass. Her eyes widened. Then she was wrenched away by a man.

* * *

When the kidnapper clasped her shoulders, Sadie screamed. He forced her lips closed them slapped a large piece of heavy-duty tape over her mouth. She kicked at him with her free leg, making several strikes in tender places before he hit her across the face.

"You're gonna regret this," he said, his voice husky as he dragged her away from the window and toward the open door, still mostly tied to the chair but twisted away so she couldn't kick him anymore.

With her back to him, she heard the sound of a low growl nearby. She turned her head at the moment Bella launched herself at the short, stocky man with his ski mask on. He dropped her against the hardwood floor next to him and took out his gun. Still sitting in the chair, tied to it, Sadie couldn't let him shoot Bella. Using all her energy, she flung herself and the attached chair against the kidnapper at the same time a shot rang out.

NINE

A blast from a gun within the house brought Brock to a standstill. Then, within a second, he whirled around and raced for the front of the place. Clay and one of his deputies used a ram against the wooden door, blocking their entry. The second time they hit the door, it flew open. Clay and his officer rushed inside with their weapons drawn.

Brock knew his friend would be angry, but there was no way he was staying outside, not after seeing Sadie briefly in the window then hearing a shot resonate through the air. He prayed she wasn't hurt.

At the entrance, he paused to assess

the situation before rushing in. To the left the elderly man who had answered their knock earlier lay on the floor not far from where Brock stood. He moved to the guy and checked his pulse.

The older gentleman's eyes popped open. "Is that thug dead?"

Brock swung his gaze to the sheriff upstairs on the landing with his gun pointed at a large man on the floor while his deputy handcuffed him and took off the kidnapper's ski mask. "I don't think so." Then he glimpsed Clay helping Sadie on the floor while Bella licked her face. Such an overwhelming relief washed over him.

"How about the lady or the dog?" The older man struggled to sit up.

Brock helped him to the nearby couch. "They're okay." At least he hoped neither one was injured. From his vantage point he couldn't tell for sure.

"Go make sure, fella. I'm fine."

Brock glanced at the gentleman. "You're sure?"

"Nothing peace and quiet won't fix. Go. I can tell they mean something to you." As

Brock turned to go upstairs, the older gentleman grabbed his arm. "Let the sheriff know there's another guy who slammed the door on you and him. He ran out the back."

Brock took the steps two at a time and hurried toward Sadie, her face buried against Bella's neck. A pile of ropes and a chair with one leg broken off lay near them. Clay assisted her to a standing position and removed tape from around her mouth.

With Bella next to her, she turned toward Brock, and he stopped in his tracks, a yard away from her. One side of her face was red and swollen as though someone used her as a punching bag. Anger swelled to the surface, and he charged toward the big guy, now on his feet standing between Clay and a deputy. He brought his arm back, intending to hit that man as the thug had Sadie.

Clay caught his fist before it made contact. "I need him in one piece to get answers. We still have two kidnappers out there and no telling who else, and we need to find Katie. And if this guy's smart," the sheriff glanced at his prisoner without his ski mask, "he'll strike a deal for a lesser crime."

"The house owner told me one of the kidnappers slammed the door in our faces then ran out the back."

"I had a deputy back there." Clay turned to the one with him. "Check on Deputy Adams. I'll take care of this one."

Brock curled his hands into balls. Neither Sadie nor Katie would be safe until the other two kidnappers were found and what was going on regarding Tom Connors' death was revealed. He glared at the suspect as he covered the distance to Sadie, petted Bella, then wrapped his arms around the only woman he'd ever fallen in love with. And yet, he had let her go because he was stubborn and prideful. He didn't want to put her through what he knew he would be dealing with.

"Are you okay?" he whispered into Sadie's ear.

She nodded. "Now that you all are here, I am. Did you get the other man? He was tall and thin."

"Do you know what he looks like?"

"No, he had a mask on the whole time. All I can tell you was he smoked cigarettes."

Clay escorted the short, bulky kidnapper out of the house.

Sadie watched them leave then stepped back from Brock's embrace and looked up at him. "Is that man downstairs the owner of this house?"

"Yes. He said he was all right. He was trying to tell us something was wrong when he was forced to answer the door."

"Good. I want to thank him."

"Me, too." Brock took her hand, needing to feel the connection between them. He'd almost lost her. With Bella following behind them, they descended the staircase.

"When the kidnappers came to my duplex, the one Clay just took outside caught me running from my place. He gave me something that knocked me out. Later the tall, thin one came upstairs where I was being kept and demanded to know where the flash drive from Mason and Fox was. I made him think I was Katie and had it somewhere other than the cabin. I was hit because I wasn't going to tell him where it was. I finally told him it was in a marked box at the duplex in my first bedroom's closet. He believed me. That means the kidnappers don't have my sister. She may be with someone else or hiding somewhere."

At the bottom of the steps, he paused and turned toward Sadie, holding both her hands and lowering his voice. "A flash drive that had something to do with the company Katie works for? I wonder why it's so important. That might be the reason why Tom Connors was murdered. I'll let Clay know, so when he's questioning the guy he took out of here, he might find out why they want it. You've only mentioned two men. There's another one. He was the driver of the car when they captured you at the duplex. I'm hoping Deputy Adams caught him as he went out back when we came."

"I have a feeling the one Clay has won't say a word, and as long as one kidnapper is out there, Katie isn't safe."

"Which means you aren't either."

She sucked in a deep breath then released it slowly. "I know. I also realize I can't go off by myself. If the news gets out that I'm not Katie, I can see them using me to get to her."

After handing the stocky assailant to a deputy, Clay returned to the house, and Brock filled him in on what the kidnappers wanted and that the tall, thin one had headed for the duplex earlier.

"You need protection, Sadie." A frown creased the sheriff's forehead. "The third man escaped. Deputy Adams ran after him through the woods but lost him."

"I agree. She can stay at my house. Simon and I can help keep her safe. She shouldn't be alone."

"I'll have a deputy outside, keeping an eye on both places. The kidnapper you sent to the duplex will figure out quickly the flash drive isn't there. The police chief is sending two of his officers to see if the suspect is still there." Clay stepped closer and scanned his surroundings. "In fact, Sadie, you need to go and check Katie's place room by room. Maybe they didn't find what they wanted before because they didn't have the time. We're looking at someone who'll do anything to get that flash drive. So far, they've murdered Connors and kidnapped you."

"You don't have to convince me. Once we find the flash drive, then maybe Katie and I will be safe.."

"At least now we know what we need to look for," Brock said while Bella nudged her way between him and Sadie.

"Before we leave, I'd like to see the gentleman who lives here." Sadie started for the old man sitting on a couch across the large room. Bella stayed right next to her.

Brock remained back to talk with Clay. "I'd like to take Sadie home now. When things start to calm down, the stress of her situation today will hit her." He'd gone through too many of those type of situations. Sadie hadn't.

"After I process this place and interview the owner, I'll come over to get Sadie's statement. I'll have Deputy Jenkins, who's coming, take you to your car parked where we started the search. Then he'll follow you to your home and stay outside in his car. I'll let you know who each one will be—all deputies you'll know."

"Thanks. I appreciate the help." Brock shook Clay's hand then crossed the room and stopped next to Sadie. He could tell she was starting to feel the adrenaline spike draining away. Her hands shook. Her shoulders slumped with exhaustion. He could see it in her eyes, too. He put his arm around her, and she didn't resist him.

Instead, she leaned against him. "I'm so glad you weren't hurt, Mr. Taylor."

"It ain't your fault. It's those three clowns who burst into my house. The deputy told me he wants me to talk to a sketch artist, but I can't help him. That skinny guy who left never took off his ski mask nor did the one who ran out the back. I hope that other goon will give up his partners."

"So do I." Sadie smiled at the gentleman as she leaned against Brock even more.

Deputy Jenkins entered the doorway.

"Time for us to leave." Brock shook the elderly man's hand. "Thank you, Mr. Taylor, for trying to warn us."

"Any time. You two stay safe."

Brock hoped Mr. Taylor's words proved to be right. At least now, they had more information about what was going on. He and Sadie headed outside.

When Brock opened the back door to the squad car, he slipped inside after Sadie, and she cuddled against his side, clasping her shaking hands. "Close your eyes. Rest," he whispered to her as her lids drooped shut.

* * *

As Sadie awakened, she hugged a pillow, relishing its softness. The mattress's comfort lured her back toward sleep. She took in a deep breath and a musky scent enveloped her. She pushed herself upright and panned the room. This wasn't her room—Brock's. The masculine furniture and touches surrounded her in a sense of safety she hadn't felt since yesterday morning before she answered her sister's call.

On the side of the bed, Bella laid her head on the coverlet beside Sadie. The dog must have been lying down on the floor while she slept.

Sadie patted the bed next to her, and Bella leaped up. The golden retriever wagged her tail while relishing the attention Sadie gave her. The fact that Bella had been in here, guarding her, rendered a few moments of forgetfulness concerning what had happened earlier. Brock and his dog made her feel safe—at least as long as she was with him. If only she hadn't gone to her house...but then she wouldn't know that Katie was most likely still alive, and the kidnappers were looking for a flash drive. And the sheriff had one of the abductors in jail. That was a lot more than they had this morning.

She buried her face against Bella. She'd found Sadie in Mr. Taylor's house. "I can see why Brock is so attached to you. You are such a good girl." She scratched the dog behind her ears. Bella wagged her tail. "We've got to go to Katie's and search her place. Are you up to helping me?"

Bella barked.

Sadie sat on the side of the bed as the golden retriever hopped down and rushed to the exit a few seconds before a knock sounded on the door. Imagining her wild look, Sadie ran her fingers through her dark red hair as she crossed the room and let Brock inside. She glanced at her watch. "It's nearly four. You should have gotten me up before now. We need to go search Katie's house."

"There are a lot of things I should do but don't. This wasn't one of them. You needed to rest. I carried you into the house. You rallied a moment when I put you on my bed, but you went right back to sleep. You crashed and wouldn't have been able to do too much until you got the rest you needed. Trust me. I know from experience."

Trust me. Those words rang through Sadie's mind. "I do, Brock. If you all hadn't come, I would have been killed. They may have worn ski masks to protect their identity as if I would be freed when I gave them what they wanted. Their ski masks didn't mean they would let me go even if I had told them where the flash drive is located, which I can't. They had only one goal, and no person was going to stand in their way. When I left to go home to check if Katie had left a message for me, I kept an eye out for any car following me. How did they find me without me knowing?"

"I don't know. Clay called me a few minutes ago. He'll be coming here after he wraps things up at the station and stops by your duplex to check the deputies' progress with your place. The one who went there after he talked to you trashed your place as though a tornado had struck. He couldn't have been there long because as soon as Clay called the Butte City Police Department, the chief sent two officers to your home. I'll call Clay and see if he's learned anything from the kidnapper he has in custody. He wanted to interview the guy before he left the station."

"Does he know who it is?"

"Yes, Jimmy Phillips. He has a record for manslaughter. He's been out of prison for a year. Supposedly a loner."

"So, no telling who his partners are. I'm assuming he hasn't said who worked with him."

"Not a word. He wants his attorney." Brock turned to leave. "I'll be in the kitchen. Simon's fixing us something to eat. I got the duffel bag at your house that you must have packed, so you'd have a few changes of clothes. I used some items to let the search dogs smell your scent. See you soon. Bella, stay with Sadie."

As he shut the door, Sadie stared at the place where he'd stood. It was as if Brock had read her mind. She wanted out of these clothes she'd worn when she was kidnapped as if shedding them would allow her to shed her memories of the ordeal. Her duffel bag sat in front of his dresser. After retrieving clean jeans and a sweatshirt, she headed into his connecting bathroom and quickly took a shower.

As she made her way to the kitchen, wearing a fresh outfit from home gave her a spring to her step. With one kidnapper arrested, they were nearer to finding out what was going on and possibly where Katie was hiding. She paused in the doorway with Bella next to her. "I'm starving. What's for lunch...or dinner?"

"Chicken salad sandwiches with chips. Nothing fancy, but I have enough for everyone to have two of them." Simon handed Sadie a bag. "We're going to eat while we search your sister's house."

She smiled. "I like that. I'm all for doing several things at the same time, especially when there's a ticking bomb threatening us, figuratively speaking, I hope."

Brock grabbed his rifle and gave Simon the shotgun. "Let's go. Katie doesn't live in a small cabin. This could take a while."

Sadie walked toward her sister's place with Brock on one side and Bella on the other. Simon was in front of her. She felt surrounded and safe, especially with a deputy sheriff watching the area.

When Sadie entered the house, seeing the place trashed again hit her as though she'd walked into a brick wall. Two of the kidnappers had done this in a short time. But they hadn't found what they wanted.

She would. "Let's eat a sandwich and then get to work."

After they ate their food and downed it with tea Simon had brought in a jug, Sadie made her way upstairs to go through Katie's room first, starting with the closet. As she stood in the mess created by her sister, she kept thinking she was forgetting something. The trauma she'd faced today was still there in the background—the kidnapper manhandling her, his foul breath, the force of his strikes.

She stared at herself in a full length mirror mounted at the end of the large walk-in closet. The redness where the kidnappers had hit her face would become bruises as if she were a boxer who had lost in the first round. After what she went through and the emotions she experienced—still did—she had a small glimpse into what Brock had experienced as a soldier in the middle of a war—fighting for others, fighting to stay alive. He'd been trained, but how could any training really prepare a person for that?

Lord, why did I let him push me away

when he needed me more than ever?

She had tried, coming to see him over and over, but he kept pushing her away. Then one day she stopped trying. She shouldn't have. It wasn't like her to give up. Was that the real reason she'd finally come back to Butte City, because she knew Brock was here? Katie occasionally would mention him and each time it felt like her heart had been squeezed.

She shook her head. She'd deal with these resurfacing feelings once she found her sister. She had to keep her focus on Katie. After she walked into the hallway and grabbed a stepladder from a storage closet, she decided to go through what was left on the shelves in the closet then put all the items on the floor back where they belonged. She positioned herself on the top step. Then she took down each box and went through it before putting it back. There were thousands of places Katie could have hidden a flash drive. This could take days. And another option was that her sister had it on her.

As that thought plagued her, Sadie kept

racking her brain for any idea where Katie would have put something that was obviously important to her. Whatever that kidnapper had given her to knock her out, it was still clouding her mind like a fog that was slowly dissipating but determined to cling as long as it could.

By the time she finished going through the items on the shelf on the left side of the closet, she descended the stepladder, stretched, and rolled her head from side to side. Her body ached from what happened earlier. In order to try to escape her captors, she'd made moves her body never had before. Her hands tremored.

She decided to go downstairs and get a glass of tea and the second sandwich. Maybe Brock and Simon were moving faster than she was. When she emerged from the closet, Bella, who had been sitting at the entrance, followed her.

Bending over the sofa, Brock checked the nooks and cracks of it. He looked up and swung his attention to her. A grin transformed his serious expression. "Did you find anything?"

She shook her head as she crossed to him."She has a big closet. More like a small room with a lot of stuff in it. How about you?"

"I didn't even find change in the couch."

Sadie scanned the living room. "At least you have half of it put back together. Where's Simon?"

"Going through the kitchen, his favorite place."

"I can't argue with that. I spend a lot of time in mine. His chicken salad is great. I'm going to have to get his recipe and another sandwich."

"Tired?"

"More than usual."

"After what you went through, that's common. I could use a sandwich, too, and Bella needs water." Brock started for the kitchen.

She would get a bowl so she could put water near Bella upstairs. She'd never seen dog so fixed on what she'd been commanded to do. The golden retriever s amazing and comforting to have rding her. No one would surprise Sadie with Bella nearby.

Simon had already grabbed the sandwiches in the refrigerator and laid them on the counter while he poured the tea into glasses. "I heard you two were hungry again and yes, Sadie, I'd be glad to give you my secret recipe for the chicken salad."

"Can I share it on my podcast? Or better yet, you can appear on it and show my followers how you make it."

Simon's cheeks reddened. "Sure." He looked from Sadie to Brock. "So far, I haven't found anything. Katie might not be too happy about me searching through the flour and sugar."

"You're being thorough. Food can be replaced. My sister can't." She held up the wrapped sandwich. "Thanks for this and your help. This will give me the energy to keep going."

Sadie left the kitchen with Brock right behind her and Bella at her side. The living room was almost put back together, and the sight gave her hope that they would find whatever the kidnappers wanted.

"What could be so important on the flash drive that people were willing to kill for it? Katie works at Mason and Fox, a shipping company."

"It's a worldwide company. They ship items in and out of this country."

"Like drugs?"

"Possibly. Or money or people."

"Human trafficking?"

Brock nodded.

"Not only is my sister's life in danger, but others could be, too." She mounted the steps. "We've got to find that flash drive."

"What if Katie has it with her?"

"It's possible, but if they found her, then they would have the flash drive and wouldn't have tried to get me to tell them where it was. If she hid it somewhere, she has a bargaining chip. That sounds more like my sister."

"Did Katie leave you a message? You never said anything about that, so I assume she didn't."

"I don't remember. So much happened the short time I was at my house. Did they find my purse? It was in my glove compartment." She patted her pockets then realized the clothes she wore earlier were at Brock's house, but she didn't remember anything about a cell phone being on her. "Most likely if my cell had been on me, the kidnappers took it. It would have been locked, though."

"I'll call Clay and see if your purse is in your car. I'll let you know what I find out," he said at the top of the staircase.

"Thanks. I should remember what I did. But all I can recall is running out the back door and being tackled by one of the kidnappers. I probably didn't have time to look for a message from my sister." She would have recalled any message from Katie, wouldn't she?

As she walked into the closet again, doubt nibbled at her. She was forgetting something. What?

After eating her sandwich in her sister's bedroom, Sadie went to work on the right top and bottom shelves, glancing occasionally at Bella on guard. It went faster because part of it was her shoe rack. Half of them were on the floor, and she would return them to their proper place while searching them for the flash drive. In the back of the top shelf at the far end, there was a box. She stood on the stool and reached for it. She was a couple of inches away, and she pushed to her tiptoes. While wobbling, she gripped the edge of the container and tumbled toward the wall at the back of the closet before putting her feet back down on the step.

She gripped a nearby metal rod where the clothes were hung. The action caused her to let go of the box. It crashed to the floor and hundreds of photos scattered everywhere. Shaken, she slowly descended and sat down. This wasn't exactly how she'd wanted to go through the box's content, but it would do.

As she looked at old photos from her childhood, her gaze latched onto one.

Like one of the games we loved to play when we were kids.

A memory flashed into her mind. She knew where her sister might have gone.

TEN

Brock finished checking the fireplace then moved to the bookcase. Every item had been thrown on the floor, strung around all of the furniture. He didn't know exactly the order they went in, but after going over the shelves, he flipped through each book then shelved them according to a category. As he put a biography in the non-fiction section, he caught sight of Sadie coming down the stairs. She had a smile on her face.

He started to say something, but the phone rang. He quickly snatched up the receiver on the nearby desk. "Hello."

"Brock, I got a message you wanted to

talk to me," the sheriff said. "Did you find something?"

"No, still going through Katie's place. Did you find Sadie's purse or her cell phone at either house?"

"I haven't gone to her place yet. A lawyer showed up to represent our suspect."

"Has he said anything to help us?"

"Clammed up and refuses to say a word." Clay's harsh laugh sounded full of sarcasm. "What's interesting is that his attorney is from a high-powered law firm in Denver, so we may never get anything out of Phillips. I'm pulling up to Sadie's duplex right now. My deputies have been processing it, so I won't stay long."

"Good. You can check for her cell phone and her purse in the glove compartment." He watched her moving across the living room toward him. Although she had a couple of hours of sleep, she still looked exhausted. "Clay, before the abduction, Sadie went to her home to see if Katie had left a message for her."

"One of my deputies checked her

landline and there weren't any messages. You need to ask her if she heard something and erased it."

"I will. She wasn't there long before the kidnappers invaded her home."

"There's something else I needed to tell you, but with all that's been going on, I forgot. We checked the calls Tom Connors made and received the day of his murder. He only called Katie, but early that morning, not the time we estimate he was killed."

"I wonder if Katie's supervisor suspected something was wrong."

"I plan to ask Katie that when she's found."

"We'll see you soon." But before Brock could say good-bye, Sadie grabbed the receiver from his hand.

"Clay, my cell phone was in the front pocket of my pants. The kidnappers must have taken it, but it would be locked so they didn't get the messages from Katie. I've been wondering how they found me. I would like you to check for a tracker on my car. I was careful about making sure a vehicle wasn't following me to my duplex, so it's got to be something like a GPS tracker that transmitted my whereabouts to the kidnappers. See you soon." Sadie hung up the receiver. "Let's go outside."

Brock faced her. "Why? We still have a lot to do."

"You're going to think me paranoid, but I need to tell you something outside. Somehow those men knew where I was this morning. It wasn't common knowledge. What if they put a GPS tracker on my car when they first showed up yesterday at Katie's? Maybe I've read too many mysteries or watched too many police shows, but we need to be cautious."

"You don't have to tell me that. Let's go out to the back deck." Brock opened the door and went first, panning the area before letting Sadie join him. When she started to say something, he put his finger up to his lips. "Wait." Then he took out his cell phone and played music, turned up as high as he could. "Your paranoia is rubbing off on me."

"Good. I got two messages from Katie

on my cell after I left my place. The first one warned me not to come to her house." She lowered her voice. "The second one said, 'Like one of the games we loved to play when we were kids.' It has to be the key because when she said the first message she was really scared. Katie witnessed Tom Connors' murder. Possibly between when she called me originally and when she left those last two messages on my cell. Her supervisor didn't live that far from her. I remember Katie telling Tom Connors about the house being for sale. He loved living on the mountain rather than in Butte City. He bought it last year. Katie really respected him."

"Okay. What games did you two like to play when you were kids?"

"There were two of them. Dad built us a treehouse through the woods behind the house. I haven't been back there in years, but it was sturdy and had several levels. It was a birthday present when we turned six. The other one was the old abandoned mine. We had a lot of adventures in both places even as teens, remember?"

"Yeah and that you always had a vivid imagination."

She nodded. "I was the one that insisted on being adventurous. Katie would come up with something practical, and I would take it to the next level. When Dad found out about the mine, he forbid us to go there. But we still did until he boarded up the entrances where the wooden planks had deteriorated."

"Then first thing tomorrow, we'll check them out. It's almost dark. We'll need to get a few things together, especially if we're going into an abandoned mine. We'll go early tomorrow morning."

Simon opened the back door. "The sheriff's on the phone, Brock."

"Okay." Brock clasped Sadie's hand and walked into the house. When he took the receiver from his younger brother, he released his hold on her and turned his back on them just in case something was wrong. Sadie knew how to read his expression better than most people. "What's going on, Clay?"

"I can't come to your place right now.

There's a forest fire on the other side of Butte City eating its way up the mountain where we rescued Sadie. I'm going to need everyone to get the people living on it or near it to evacuate. If we get enough people to fight the fire, we have a good chance of stopping it before it really spreads. If the wind increases and changes its direction, you all on your mountain will have to be evacuated, too, not to mention possibly all of the town residents. If that happens, I'll let you know. I was going to relieve Deputy Jenkins with someone who hasn't worked all day, but I can't spare anyone. He wants to stay. For the time being, he will, but I may even need him if the fire spreads rapidly."

"Go. I understand. We'll probably work another hour then try to get some rest, so we can finish up tomorrow if the wind hasn't shifted." Brock felt the tension stiffen Sadie's body. "We'll be okay. At least for the time being, the winds aren't too strong. Hopefully, it can be contained right away." When he ended the call, he turned toward Sadie and Simon, who were both staring at him.

She frowned. "What's wrong?"

"There's a fire on the mountain where you were found today. We're on our own for the time being." He told both of them what Clay had said. "There's even a chance he'll need Deputy Jenkins if the fire gets worse and spreads fast. We need to listen to the news and the forecast."

"Does he think this was set by the other kidnappers?"

"Clay didn't say, and I don't think anyone knows how it started. But it's a possibility. I think we have to act as though it was."

Simon shook his head as though he couldn't believe what was going on. "Whatever Katie knows must be big. Someone is going through a lot to get the information back."

Sadie wrote on a pad near the phone. "I think we need to stay here and keep looking for the flash drive, at least as long as we can, but remember to act as though this place has been bugged."

Simon nodded along with Brock who

said, "Let's see how our search goes."

Sadie started for the stairs. "I don't think there's anything here. A few more hours and we'll know one way or the other."

Brock grinned and winked at her as she went up the steps. He didn't think Katie left the flash drive here because she was rushing to get away and knew it would be only a matter of time before these killers came after her. She would take her leverage with her, and if she hid the flash drive, it was somewhere else—possibly the place where Sadie and her twin played as youngsters or the cave where he'd joined them as a teen.

* * *

Hours later, Sadie backed out of the walk-in closet, positive there wasn't anywhere inside it that she hadn't checked. She even looked into all the pockets on the clothes, and Katie had a lot, but she'd also remembered the loose baseboard in the back corner. That would have been a perfect place, except nothing but dust balls as well as a photo of her and Katie one Christmas, standing in front of the decorated tree, were behind the floorboard. They had been ten and had hidden the picture there—and had obviously forgotten about it.

Bella had been lying by the left side of the entrance into the closet. She lumbered to her feet while Sadie took another step back into a solid wall of muscles. For a split second, she thought it was one of the kidnappers who were still at large. Then she got a whiff of a musky scent and relaxed. Brock clasped her shoulders and pulled her against him."I finished the living room, dining room and office. Nothing. After searching the kitchen, Simon went through the other two bedrooms up here. He's going through the upstairs bathroom right now."

"Good. You can help me with the one connected to this bedroom. That's all I have left. I was just making sure I thought of every place in this monster-sized closet. When this house was being built, my mother insisted on a big one. What time is it?" She turned to look at the clock on the nightstand. "Two in the morning! Time speeds by when you're having so much fun."

Brock chuckled and winked at her. "Is that what it is?"

"Well, at least once we finish with the bathrooms, we can go back to your place and get some rest. The flash drive isn't here."

"Maybe Katie never had whatever those men were looking for."

"She didn't say anything to me, and she always shares everything with me."

His eyes widened. He took her hand and pulled her into the bathroom where he turned on the water. Leaning toward her, he whispered, "If they bugged this place, be careful. I don't want the kidnappers to think she shared something else with you. Like the fact she witnessed Connors' murder."

She never thought about that. "Let's get this done and go back to your house."

He nodded and turned off the nozzle.

"That cold water felt good. I needed it to keep me awake long enough to finish."

Within fifteen minutes, they completed the search and met Simon coming out of the main bathroom. "Nothing here."

"Let's go." Brock headed for the staircase.

As Sadie left her family home, she realized she would never feel safe in this place again even if the other kidnappers were found—nor would she in her duplex.

Outside, Sadie, surrounded by Bella, Simon, and Brock, hurried to his home. The stench of smoke filled the air, but she didn't see any flames in the sky because the heavy trees around them blocked the view. The wind, stronger than earlier, came from the direction of the fire.

At the entrance, Brock paused. "I'm going to talk to Deputy Jenkins and see what's happening with the fire. Be back soon."

Sadie entered the house first with Bella right behind her and then Simon, who shut and locked the door.

"Are you hungry?" he asked as he

walked toward the kitchen.

"Yes."

"I'll find something to make that isn't a sandwich since that's all we've been eating."

"I'd even take one of your chicken salad sandwiches. Do you need help?"

"Nope. Sit and relax."

"I'm afraid if I did, I'd never get up." She started for the kitchen.

The front door opened. Although she knew it had to be Brock, she froze. Flashbacks to the men breaking into her home this morning held her captive as though it were on a loop that wouldn't stop running.

"Sadie?"

The kidnapper's fingers grasping her felt like talons digging into her flesh. She shuddered.

"Sadie, you're safe here." Brock moved in front of her and slowly reached for her.

She fixed her gaze on him, but the shivering flooding her wouldn't stop.

He stepped closer. "I'm here. I know what you're going through. The trauma you experienced this morning isn't something you'll get over right away."

Tears blurred her vision. Through the watery haze, she saw his kindness and a connection she hadn't experienced in years. "I've never felt so vulnerable in my life. I thought I was going to die. I couldn't give them the information they wanted."

"But now you aren't alone. I'm here. Bella and Simon, too. I'll do whatever I have to in order to protect you."

The tension in her body began to drain from her. She closed the few inches between them and wrapped her arms around him, clinging to him as though he were a life raft. And in this moment, he definitely was. She laid her head against his chest over his heart and listened to its beating—a soothing and comforting sound. She didn't want to move from his embrace.

Behind Brock, Simon cleared his throat. "I hate to interrupt, but the scrambled eggs will get cold if you don't eat them soon."

Sadie reluctantly dropped her arms while Brock leaned close to her ear and whispered, "We'll pick this up after we eat."

Then he backed away a few inches and turned toward his brother. "It smells delicious."

As they sat at the table and ate an early breakfast, every time she looked at Brock, her heartbeat raced. What were they going to pick up after they finished the meal?

"What did the deputy say?" Simon passed the plate with strips of bacon on it.

"We may have to evacuate, depending on the force of the wind and how well the firefighters can contain the fire. The forecast is that the wind will get stronger by tomorrow morning." Brock took a bite of his scrambled eggs.

"Then we need to pray it doesn't. When we walked back over here, I thought the wind had picked up. If Katie is out there somewhere, hiding, she might not realize the fire could take hold of this mountain. It just takes a strong wind carrying a spark to ignite one. We've got to find her in case it does get worse over the next couple of days."

"You're right." Brock bowed his head and asked, "Lord, please protect the people in the path of this fire, the ones who are fighting to contain it, and Katie wherever she is. Help us to find her and stop whoever is behind this. Amen."

Sadie sighed. "I hope we locate her because other than those two places, I don't have any idea where she might be. Since her car hasn't been found, maybe she's miles and miles away from here." She hoped the last was true, but in her gut, she didn't think that was the case. Maybe she moved her car to draw the assailants away from this area. There were dense woods on the mountain and deep ravines where a car could be hidden from view. When thinking about some of the drop-offs on the highway, what if Kate skidded off the road because of the rain and went off the side of the mountain? She could be hurt—or dead. She pushed that thought from her mind. She needed to be positive. They would find Katie alive wherever she was.

"If we can't find her, hopefully, the people hunting her can't either." Brock cupped her hand that rested on the table.

The gesture reminded her she wasn't

alone, and right now she needed that. She turned her hand over and clasped his. Their physical connection calmed some of the anxiety trying to discourage her.

When they finished their meal, Simon said, "I'll take care of the dishes."

In the living room, Brock paused. "I want you to sleep upstairs. Simon and I will be down here."

"You've got to get rest, too."

"We'll be sleeping on the two couches. Bella's a great watchdog, and Deputy Jenkins' wife brought him a big thermos of coffee and dinner earlier. He assured me he's wide awake."

"We need to leave as soon as it's light."

"I agree. My watch has an alarm. I'll set it." Brock stepped into her personal space and grasped her hands, tugging her against him. "We'll find her. If the places we're going to check don't pan out, then we'll keep looking. We'll scour the area."

"Thanks. I don't know what would have happened if you hadn't come over yesterday morning."

His large hands framed her face. "You

asked me to. I'm not the same person I was four years ago in the hospital bed, angry at the world and feeling like the future I'd planned was out of my reach."

"You shouldn't have given up on me."

"I know. But I'd given up on myself at that time. I didn't have it in me. I thought the best thing I could do for you was for us to go our separate ways. Now I realize I wasn't thinking things through, clearly not taking in your concerns as well as mine."

She didn't know what to say. The love she had for him was still there in her heart, but she'd promised herself she would never again go through the pain caused by his words spoken four years ago. She had flown to Germany to be there for him. At first, she'd been told he might never regain consciousness. It had been touch and go for several days. Then when he finally awakened and could see visitors, all she could think of was holding him and telling him how much she loved him and would be there for him.

Sadie stepped back. "I should go to sleep."

Before she moved further away from him, Brock closed the space and wrapped his arms around her. "I've wanted to say that to you for a while." He leaned forward and brushed his lips across hers.

She started to pull away. Instead, she locked her arms around him and really kissed him for the first time in years. All the buried emotions rose to the surface, demanding release, and Sadie couldn't stop herself. She poured herself into the caress of her mouth against his—as though she'd come home, finally.

Then her conflicting feelings swamped her as if she'd been pulled in two different directions. The pain of the past invaded her and took over. She pushed away from him, spun around, and raced up the stairs.

On the second-floor landing, she glanced back.

He started for her.

"Don't." That one word held all her anguish.

He halted.

She continued down the hall and collapsed on his bed. She drew part of the coverlet over her and curled into a ball. In that second, she felt as though she were Katie, huddled in a dark space, shivering.

ELEVEN

When Brock's alarm sounded, he groaned, wishing he'd gotten more sleep. He'd tossed and turned the whole three hours. Pushing to a sitting position, he panned the living room. The couch across the room was empty. Where was Simon? As Brock sat up, his brother came in from the kitchen, carrying the shotgun and backpack.

"I made sandwiches in case we're gone a long time."

Brock stood. "Good thinking."

"While I was falling asleep last night, I heard you talking to Clay. Any news about the fire or the kidnappers?"

"The fire is spreading but not as fast as earlier. The winds are dying down, and the firefighters are hopeful they can contain it."

"That's good. We won't have to worry about that. Now if only the other two kidnappers can be found."

Even if they found them, would that be the end of what was happening right now? Someone probably hired those thugs to come after Katie. He'd deal with that once they found Sadie's sister. He glanced at a window with streams of light coming through between the slats in the shade. "I'll go wake up Sadie. We need to leave as soon as possible."

He headed for the stairs, not only needing to wake Sadie, but to get supplies that might come in handy in a cave. He also must consider what was going on not far from here. A wildfire could shift directions quickly. He didn't want to be unprepared.

At the door to his bedroom, he knocked, and seconds later, Sadie opened it. Circles under her eyes indicated she hadn't slept well either.

"Are you all right?" Brock wanted to pull her to him and hold her, but there wasn't any time.

"I didn't get any rest. I kept feeling..." Her eyebrows scrunched together, and she crossed her arms over her chest.

"Feeling what?"

"Katie and how scared she is. We've always had a close bond. What if the other kidnappers found her? We could be too late."

"We're leaving as soon as I get my backpack."

She moved to the side to let him into his bedroom. "I'm going to turn on the TV and see if there's an update on the fire."

"Good idea. I'll be ready in a few minutes. We'll leave out the back door."

"Did you tell Deputy Jenkins what we're going to do?"

"No, but after you went to bed last night, I told Clay."

"About the cave?"

"No, only that we're going to search the area around Katie's house in case she's hiding somewhere."

Sadie turned and walked down the hallway with Bella next to her.

He'd been wrong to let her go because he'd been scared about how he would deal with losing part of a leg and surviving when many of his combat buddies had died. The memory of that day in the hospital flooded his mind. The look on her face tore at the emotional barrier that he'd erected around him. After she'd left, he'd tried to get out of the bed and collapsed to the floor. Lying on the cold linoleum, struggling to get up and reach the call button, had only reinforced all the reasons he should let Sadie go.

Brock quickly entered his room and opened his closet where he kept his backpack and certain items he might need—night vision goggles and a headlamp for the cave, several flashlights, extra ammunition for both guns, and wool blankets in case the fire flared back up and jumped to this mountain. In that case, they would need some kind of protection.

When he pivoted to leave, his gaze fell onto his bed. The only evidence Sadie had been there was the tussled coverlet as though she had fought it all night long. He'd done his share of wrestling with his own demons while trying to sleep. Many times, he'd lost the battle until Bella had become a part of his life and was there to stop those nightmares before they took over.

He shook those thoughts from his mind and made his way downstairs to the living room. "Let's go."

Simon exchanged backpacks with Sadie. "The food isn't as heavy as the water."

She gave him a smile then crossed to the rear exit and paused. "On the TV, the reporter said the fire was contained a couple of hours ago on Black Bear Mountain, so we should be okay here."

"Good." Brock hurried and opened the door. "If you get tired, I can carry my pack and yours."

"No, I can do this. I understand you didn't sleep much either." Sadie hiked her chin.

Simon pressed his lips together as though he were trying not to grin.

Brock shot his little brother a dagger look. "I'm fine. I don't require much." He pulled the door open and let Simon leave first and then Sadie with Bella.

He quickly joined them on the deck and went ahead to the steps then lifted his binoculars from around his neck. He surveyed the terrain before them, pausing a couple of times to make sure no one was hiding behind a thick tree trunk or a thicket of greenery. The stench of smoke lingered in the air. The wind wasn't as strong as it had been last night. He was thankful that the fire had been contained. Weather and fast action had made that possible. He hoped no one was hurt or homes burned down. Except for the rain the other day, they hadn't had any in two months, so things were dry.

When he put the binoculars down, he glanced back at Sadie and Simon. "We need to spread out with Sadie and Bella in the middle. We have to remain in sight of each other. We'll cover more ground that way."

"Are we going to the treehouse?" Sadie

petted Bella and clipped her leash onto the golden retriever's collar.

"Yes. After that, I'll have Bella smell one of Katie's shirts and see if she can pick up her scent. I want to be further away from her house before we do that. Usually she doesn't spend a lot of time in the woods behind her place," Brock said as he started in the direction of the treehouse.

He kept his focus on his surroundings. He'd told Sadie he'd protect her, and he would fulfill that promise. He'd let her down once and couldn't again. She needed to feel safe with all that had been going on the past few days. She glanced at him. For a few seconds, he glimpsed fear in her eyes, but she quickly looked away.

When Sadie reached the treehouse, Brock and Simon joined her beneath it. The pieces of wood that had been nailed on the trunk to serve as a ladder were gone. Even the rope that used to dangle from the entrance into the secret place was missing.

"Katie," Sadie said in a soft voice then again louder. "I was hoping she was here and had destroyed the way to get up inside."

"It doesn't give her as much cover, and it's still close to her house." Brock clasped her shoulder, feeling the tension beneath his palm. "The cave would be a better hiding place."

Sadie swung her attention to him. "What if she isn't there either?"

"We'll keep looking. With the fire under control, Clay will have more men to help search for Katie and the two kidnappers. Soon it will get rockier and have less tree cover, so we can spread out a little more. Let's go." Brock took out the shirt and held it for his dog to smell. "Bella, find."

His golden retriever sniffed the air and took off up the mountain. He prayed she was onto something.

Forty minutes later, they arrived at the entrance into the cave. The crisscrossed boards across the front stopped Bella. She sat and barked.

"My sister must be in the cave."

Simon waved his arm toward the obstruction across the front. "How did she get inside?"

Brock began testing the two-by-fours. One was loose, and he easily pulled it off. "It's a tight squeeze. Sadie and you shouldn't have too much trouble, but I'll have to take another one off."

Once Brock removed a second piece of wood and had the headlamp secured on his forehead, they entered the cave. Then he, with Simon's help. put the two-by-fours back in place.

"Bella's tugging on the leash." Sadie moved further into the darkness and toward the main corridor of the mine. Even in here, she could smell the smoke in the air that hung over the town and the mountains surrounding the area. The same thing had happened years ago when there had been a wildfire near Butte City and the wind carried the stench.

"Katie," she called out. When she didn't hear anything, she took several steps forward and yelled her sister's name.

Silence was the only thing that greeted Sadie. Her shoulders drooped. "I was hoping she would be right here." She stared at the blackness before her and tried to remember the layout of the mine. It had been years since she'd been in here.

Brock came up behind her and encircled his arms around her. "If she's in here, we'll find her."

"If she was in here, she would have called out when I did."

"This mine is big."

She sagged against him. "Until now, I forgot how big it was. To me as a child, it just meant a lot of adventures to explore."

"I'll be here with you. I've got a flashlight for everyone, but I only want two on at a time. I'll go first and hold onto Bella's leash. You'll be second while Simon will take up the rear. Keep your light off for the time being. At each tunnel that leads off the main one, we'll call out for Katie. I'll go down it a few yards. If Bella doesn't indicate she's been there, then I'll turn around, and we'll continue down the main shaft." Brock backed away, dug through his pack, and passed a flashlight to her and then Simon.

As she followed Brock, she missed his arms being around her. When she had planned to return to Butte City last month, she'd refused to acknowledge that Brock's presence here had anything to do with her decision, which was her first warning things weren't what she tried to convince herself they were. She'd kept telling herself she could manage to avoid him, even with the fact he lived next door to her twin. She knew a few of the longtime neighbors who still lived in the area near Katie. She could have called one of them to check on her sister. No, she immediately phoned Brock and had been disappointed when he hadn't answered. That should have been her second warning that she hadn't stopped loving him even after what happened in the hospital room in Germany. Her third sign was that she was here with Brock, and she trusted him with her life.

In the first three offshoot tunnels, Brock returned to the main one after only a few minutes. She began to worry about Katie. When they were kids, Sadie had always been the one who wanted to explore more of the cave. She'd always done it because the dark unknown didn't bother her. But

Katie had always been a little hesitant."Brock, do you see anything like footprints that might be Katie's?"

He leaned his head down and slowed his pace. "No. This floor is mostly stone with little dust or dirt on it. Besides, there's a draft blowing through here. If there were any, they wouldn't have stayed long."

"I don't know about you guys, but it seems like the wind is picking up and the stench of smoke is getting stronger. Not to mention the cave is getting cooler. I should have brought a heavier coat," Simon said.

The main shaft was going down into the mountain. Sadie glanced back at Simon, not far behind her. "Sometimes in the spring and fall, it gets cold in here, especially with the wind blowing through the cave. Not too far ahead is an are alike a large room that opens up with five tunnels off of it. It might be warmer there."

"I remember a couple of those shafts were narrow and didn't go too far. When this was mined for silver over a hundred years ago, the miners would dig into a tunnel. When the silver petered out, they stopped digging, which is why some shafts don't go very far. This place was owned by two brothers."

"I'm surprised you researched the origins of this cave, Brock."

"I didn't. Your sister did and mentioned it to me once."

Sadie chuckled. "That's Katie. She always wanted to know everything she could about a place." She remembered once when they took a Caribbean cruise together. Katie learned everything she could about the ship's stops. They never went on a planned excursion trip because her sister became Sadie's tour guide in each country where they docked.

A few minutes later, Brock paused in the entrance of the large cavern with the five tunnels branching off.

Sadie stopped on his right side and surveyed the area. "Katie. Are you here?"

Silence, except for the sound of water dripping.

Sadie moved to the nearest stalagmite and checked behind the rock formation coming up from the floor. No Katie. She went to the next one and inspected all of them as she circled the expanse.

Brock approached her. "It's been years. Which tunnels are a dead end?"

Sadie turned slowly pointing out three.

"I'll circle the room and see what Bella does." When his golden retriever sniffed the air and tugged on her leash to go down the third tunnel first, Brock said, "I'll take a look. You stay here with Simon."

"No. I'm coming with you."

He gave her a lopsided grin. "Somehow, I knew you would say that. Simon, guard our backs."

Simon inspected the area and planted himself between the wall of the room and a large stalagmite. He held his shotgun in front of him.

Seeing his stance reminded Sadie of the danger that surrounded them. They had to locate Katie before the kidnappers found her. Just because Bella was following her sister's scent didn't mean Katie was still in the cave. She could have been here and left.

Sadie stepped up to the shaft Bella had

indicated and called out, "Katie, this is Sadie."

Not a sound in response.

Brock moved around Sadie and held her sister's shirt in front of Bella then took her off her leash. "Find Katie."

Sniffing the air, the dog trotted down the tunnel. Brock increased his pace to keep up with her and give her light. While Sadie was right behind him, he tried to keep an eye on Bella, who disappeared around a curve in the shaft.

A bark reverberated through the passageway.

Sadie flipped on her flashlight and hurried around Brock. Her pace increased as she went around the bend. She first saw Bella sitting then in another step, she spied Katie on the floor.

Huddled in a ball. Not moving.

TWELVE

Sadie rushed toward her sister, nearly stumbling over a rock in her path. She used the side of the cave to steady herself then kept going, her heart beating so fast she could hardly draw air into her lungs. As she knelt, she reached out to feel the side of Katie's neck. Her pulse pounded slowly against her fingertips.

"What's wrong with her?" She carefully rolled Katie onto her back, so she could see where she was hurt. When Sadie's gaze zeroed in on a bump over her sister's left eye, she leaned close to Katie's mouth to see if she was breathing. *Yes!*

Brock ran his hands down Katie's body.

When he touched her right ankle beneath her jeans, Katie flinched and moved.

Sadie looked at Brock. "What's wrong?"

"Her ankle's swollen." Brock scanned the area around them. "She must have fallen, hit her head, and lost her flashlight." He pointed at its broken pieces a couple of yards away.

A groan escaped Katie's mouth. Her eyelids slowly lifted, and she wet her lips. "What day...is it?"

Sadie blew out a long breath of relief. "Friday. We've been looking for you for two days."

"What happened to you?" Her sister stared at Sadie's black eye, no doubt getting worse looking since yesterday.

"I ran into the guys who are after you."

Katie tried to sit up, but she sank back against the floor, another moan filling the air.

Sadie quickly put her hand under her sister's head to cushion it while she reached for Katie's backpack a couple of feet away to use as a pillow. "We'll talk about what's going on when we get you help." She glanced at Brock then back at her twin. "Can you get up?"

"I tried...Fell again. Water?"

Brock quickly uncapped a fresh bottle of the liquid. "Drink slowly." He stood. "I'm going to need Simon to help carry you out of here. Don't try to stand again without help."

"Yes, sir," Katie said with a brief smile then took another gulp of water.

While Brock left, Sadie asked, "Did you pass out?"

"I don't think so." Katie paused a few seconds. "Maybe. I don't know."

"I called your name several times. You didn't hear me."

"I fell. I might have passed out then, but I came to and managed to get up, only to fall again when I put full pressure on my right ankle. I collapsed. My flashlight flew out of my hand as I tried to stop myself. Everything went dark. I was exhausted and afraid to try to leave again. After hours in the dark, I must have fallen asleep." Her sister's eyes fluttered closed.

"Katie, stay awake." When she opened

her eyes, Sadie inspected her sister's ankle. "It doesn't look good."

"It doesn't feel good either." Again Katie closed her eyes but opened them a few seconds later.

Sadie's concern multiplied. Katie was hurt and those kidnappers were still out there looking for her.

After Brock returned with Simon, they discussed how best to move Katie. Sadie picked up the plastic pieces of her sister's flashlight and stuffed them into her backpack.

"Let's form a chair with our arms and carry her out that way. I think the tunnels are wide enough. Sadie and Bella can go ahead of us, holding the light. I have my headlamp on, so I can use my hands." He turned it on for the first time, thankful he'd remembered it as part of their provisions.

Sadie took Katie's backpack and Simon's shotgun because he didn't have a strap on the weapon to sling over his shoulder like his brother could. Brock fixed his rifle across his back then squatted down on the right side of Katie while Simon did the same on the left. After Brock clasped his brother's wrists, supporting her twin's shoulder and under her knees, they slowly rose with Katie between them.

"Sadie, let us know if the path isn't smooth or if there's something that might make us stumble."Brock looked at her with such a soft expression as he had when they had been dating and he'd told her he loved her.

For a few seconds while Brock and Simon made sure Katie was secured between them, a memory she'd always shoved out of her mind these past four years when she began to think of Brock intruded into her thoughts. A month before he was deployed to the war zone, they hiked to their special place at the top of this mountain where the view was indescribable, particularly that day. He got down on one knee, opened a small box, and asked her to marry him. For once, she had been speechless until his forehead scrunched, and he began to stand up as though he'd thought she didn't want to be his wife.

"Sadie, are you okay?" Brock asked. "We're ready to leave."

"Yeah." Shaking the memory from her thoughts, she turned forward and headed toward the large cavern. The only tunnel that was tricky was this narrow, dead-end one. Brock had to turn sideways and lead the way with Katie.

With Bella at her side, Sadie lit the way, occasionally glancing over her shoulder to see how the trio was doing. Katie looked exhausted and in pain. But the important thing was Sadie had her sister back. *Thank You, Lord.*

When they entered the large room, Sadie blew out a long breath. The tunnel they'd left was the riskiest one. The rest would be a lot easier. She headed toward the shaft that led to the exit. As she got closer to the mine's entrance, the scent of smoke worsened. In the illumination of her flashlight, particles of smoke hung in the glow, denser toward the ceiling.

Sadie shivered not because she was cold, but something was wrong. She stopped and pivoted.

Katie coughed, her asthma irritated by the smoke. Her eyes glistened.

"The smoke is worse than when we came in." Sadie grasped Katie's backpack and dug through it, hoping to find Katie's inhaler. Her sister hadn't packed it. Sadie would save the scolding for later. Katie had other things on her mind when trying to flee.

"I know, Sadie," Brock said. "Go ahead and check what's happening. My flashlight will give us enough light."

She hurried toward the cave's entrance. The smoke was so thick she could barely see the opening. When she reached it, the wind blew at least twice as strong than it had when they'd come into the cave. The gray veil thickened so much she couldn't see the trees a hundred yards away. She removed the two loose boards and moved a few feet away from the exit. The only good thing about the situation was she had to step outside the mine to feel the full force of the gusts and to see even thicker smoke than what was in the cave.

Coughing, she reentered, her tearing

eyes stinging. "There must be a fire nearby, most likely on this mountain. The wind is coming from the northwest. The cave's opening faces full north."

Both Brock and Simon squatted and placed Katie on the floor where the smoke wasn't as heavy. They stood and stretched while her sister coughed over and over.

Sadie paced. "There used to be a back way out of this cave facing northeast, but it wouldn't be easy getting Katie out of that exit. It's really narrow."

"I think it's still there. I saw it a few months ago when hiking." Brock pulled out Katie's shirt, which he'd used for Bella to smell, dumped a bottle of water on the material, then handed it to Sadie's twin. "Tie it around your nose and mouth."

"Back in the large cavern, the smoke wasn't as bad," Katie said, her words muffled behind her mask.

Sadie squatted next to her twin. "We could retreat to it. If conditions worsen there, we could use the rear exit. We can drag Katie through the tunnel if she can't do it on her own. If this is a wildfire, the rocky terrain around us will help keep this area from fueling the fire and making it a lot worse, which will help the firefighters contain it."

Brock nodded. "True. There isn't any fuel in this cave. If there's a fire on this mountain coming uphill, it'll be moving fast, especially with the wind. We don't know which way to go, so being in a place that's barren of fuel might be the best choice." He looked from one person to the next.

"Yes," Simon said and strode to the exit. He stepped outside but rushed back within a minute. "I can see flames below us. We need to get moving."

"I agree. We can't outrun a wildfire, especially going uphill." Sadie hated seeing her sister having trouble breathing, especially in conditions that would make it worse, but they didn't have a choice. They needed to hunker down. "If the other fire was contained on the other mountain, then how did this one start?"

"It only takes a spark in a remote place then toss in wind and you have a fire that can get out of control fast."Brock bent down on one side of Katie while Simon did on the other. "We need to move deeper into the cave. I'm glad that smoke rises. We'll find a place with a high ceiling that doesn't have as much smoke and get low on the ground."

"And pray," Sadie murmured, beginning to wonder if the people looking for Katie had something to do with this wildfire. She needed to think the worse and be prepared, especially after what happened to her yesterday.

Once Brock and Simon rose with Katie cradled between them, Sadie and Bella led the way back to the large cavern. They crossed it to the other side, near where the water was dripping from several stalactites and filling a hole in the ground. The men put Katie on the floor near the small pool on the far side of the room, out of the way of the two main shafts, which faced each other and where the wind from outside was the strongest in the cave.

"I have two wool blankets if we need to wet them and huddle under them. Wool is a retardant which should help us. I don't think the fire will flash through the tunnels, but I'd rather be prepared in case it does. As it passes over this area, the smoke density will lessen, especially near the ground, and then we can escape down the mountain."

While they prepared for a flashover, the air heated up. The smoke thickened. Sadie helped Katie lay on the floor. Sadie did her best to cushion her sister's bruised head and swollen ankle from the hard surface beneath her. Brock wetted one blanket and passed it to Simon who put it over Katie and him while Brock soaked up the rest of the water with the second cover. With Bella against her front, Sadie spooned against Brock who threw one arm over her and nestled against her back. His nearness sent her heart pounding.

No matter how much she'd tried to forget Brock after he broke off their engagement, she could never do it. She never stopped loving him in spite of what happened between them four years ago.

"We're going to be okay," he whispered

into Sadie's ear. "Lord, help us."

"Amen."

Sweat rolled into her eyes while she tried to inhale shallow breaths of the foul air. The sound of Katie coughing stiffened Sadie's resolve to get her twin help as quickly as possible, even in spite of the thugs hunting them. If she had to pretend to be her sister to keep them away from Katie, Sadie would.

* * *

Fifteen minutes later, Brock peeled back the wet blanket and surveyed the situation. Smoke still hung around the stalactites on the cavern's ceiling but not as dense. He sat up and looked around. "Smoke is dissipating. Stay here while I go check outside the cave. If it looks safe, we'll leave. I'll hurry. Stay down until I come back."

With his rifle in hand, Brock moved fast through the main tunnel to the opening. He approached the way out cautiously. He couldn't shake the feeling the assailants hunting Katie set the fire to flush them out. Had the wildfire yesterday been a diversion or an accident? He was at least thankful it had been contained quickly. Having lived in Colorado for years, he knew how a fire could spread out of control before firefighters arrived. He prayed the one on this mountain could be contained as fast as the one last night on Black Bear Mountain.

He peered out the side of the cave and could still smell the smoke, but the air was a lighter gray, much better than forty minutes ago. Off in the distance, he spied a few firefighters checking for any hotspots that needed to be taken care of. He turned and hurried back to the other three. With firefighters around the area, Katie could get the medical attention needed. He was more concerned about the bump on her head than the ankle. She said she went to sleep, but she could have been unconscious.

When he reentered the cavern, he said, "We're leaving here. There are firefighters around looking for hot pockets that need to be taken care of. Katie, they can call for medical help, but often they have paramedics nearby with a wildfire."

Sadie aided her sister as she sat up. Katie's face was pale in stark contrast to the dark circles under her eyes and the knot on her forehead. Sadie looked at Brock with fear. He'd seen it on soldiers' faces who were afraid one of their comrades was in serious trouble.

Brock covered the distance to her. "Katie, are you ready for us to carry you?"

She closed her eyes and dropped her head forward.

Brock knelt next to her. "Katie?"

She slowly looked at him, blinking and scanning their faces. "What?"

"We're carrying you out of here. Okay?" He didn't like seeing her confusion and slow response to his question.

"I'm...okay." She slurred the words together.

Another sign she probably had a concussion. Brock caught Sadie's attention. "We need to go now. We'll do what we did before as quickly as we can safely." When he turned his focus on her sister, he continued, "Katie, we're going to try to keep you from being jostled." She looked away as if she didn't hear him."Katie, you have signs of a concussion. We might have to move slower."

"I'm...fine." Again, Katie's words came out jumbled.

Brock and Simon formed another chair with their arms and carefully lifted Katie as though they moved as one.

Sadie wetted the shirt again and placed it around her sister's face then led the procession with Bella. The main tunnel toward the entrance held less smoke, but what remained still caused Katie to cough several times, which jostled her head.

Light entered the cave's opening. "I'm going ahead to see if I can flag down a firefighter. I can figure out how to use this shotgun I'm carrying if the kidnappers are out there. I can aim it and pull the trigger," Sadie said.

Brock frowned. "I don't like that. We aren't that far, and we still don't know where the kidnappers are or what they look like."

Sadie wanted to do something to help

her sister. Brock saw her at war with wanting to go ahead or listening to him. She'd already put herself in danger when she acted on feelings rather than stopping to think of the consequences of her action by going to her house to see if Katie had left her a message. Her sister thought everything out while Sadie had always been the impulsive one. Now she needed to listen to him. When she didn't go ahead, he exhaled a long breath. In that moment, he realized he loved her—even the impulsive side of her.

When they neared the exit, Brock glimpsed two men in fire gear waving at a nearby group of three a little further away. "Sadie, don't go any further. Let me check these guys out."

She stopped and moved a few steps back while Brock and Simon placed Katie on the ground. Sadie knelt next to her sister, leaning against a wall of an alcove. Sadie held her twin's hand.

Brock positioned himself on the right side of the entrance, keeping himself hidden in the dark shadows while he used his binoculars to check out the two firefighters still slowly progressing toward the cave. The trio nearby moved away. The height of the two firefighters were similar to the two kidnappers. With their fire gear on and masks, Brock couldn't tell what they looked like. The trio walking away had their hats on but nothing covering their face. Also, the two guys walked past a hotspot and didn't do anything. Doubt nibbled at him. He didn't have a good feeling about this.

But Katie needed help. Was he overreacting? He focused his binoculars on the taller man. He'd paused and watched the three firefighters for a moment. When the guy turned to the side, Brock glimpsed a gun's handle sticking out of his backpack. If the kidnappers set this fire to flush Katie out, these two could be those culprits. Every instinct he'd developed as a soldier told him not to seek help with the couple still watching the trio of rescuers leaving.

He hurried back to Sadie, Simon, and Katie. "There's a chance two guys dressed as firefighters are the kidnappers. I think one of them is carrying a gun. I couldn't tell about the other guy. There are other people in the area. To be on the safe side, we need to get to them rather than the two nearby."

"With those two out front, how?" Simon asked.

"I—have…" Katie patted her pocket and looked at Sadie. "They can't…" Her sister's eyes closed. "Fla—sh—drive." The last couple of slurred words were drawn out.

Sadie withdrew the flash drive. "I've got it. Don't worry about it anymore." She glanced at Brock. "I look like Katie. If those guys see me, they'll think I'm Katie. You and I can draw them away from her and Simon."

"By running out of the cave?" Simon asked.

Brock shook his head. "No, we're going to draw them into the cave. If they see Sadie, they'll follow us, and we can escape out of the back exit. You and Katie will stay hidden in that first tunnel off the main shaft. It's not far from the exit."

His brother frowned. "What if they

check each tunnel?"

"You'll have the shotgun. If that happens, there's a curve in the tunnel, and you can use that as a shield. I can come back, and we'll have them surrounded. But I don't intend for them to do that. Sadie, you'll briefly show yourself in the entrance then start moving quickly through the tunnels to the rear exit with Bella. Have her bark several different times the first ten minutes, so the kidnappers will go past Katie and Simon. They'll be focused on Bella's barking. I'll be right behind you not too far back. If I have to take a stand, don't stop. Keep going. Get out of the cave and find help."

Sadie released her sister's hand. "What about Katie?"

"Simon, you'll need to decide whether to walk her out of here by supporting most of her weight or wait for help to come." Brock turned his attention to Katie. "How do you feel?"

"O–kay."

"Let's do this." Sadie hugged her sister then stood and took Bella's leash.

Brock rose with Katie between him and Simon, and they moved her to the passageway off the main shaft with Sadie leading the way.

After making sure Simon and Katie were settled, Brock headed back to the main tunnel. Sadie followed with Bella.

"When you come back in the mine, leave your light off, Sadie. Keep Bella on a leash. She'll be able to see better in the dark and can lead you."

"How are you going to see?"

"I have my night vision goggles and intend to use them to my advantage." He walked with her to the end of the offshoot from the primary shaft. Before she stepped out into the larger passage and gave the kidnappers a glimpse of her at the mine's opening, he caught her arm and stopped her.

She shifted toward him. "I'll be careful."

He cupped her face, seeing her barely in the faint light from the cave's entrance. "Don't come back for me even if you think something's wrong. I can take care of myself. Your goal is to get out of here and find help and get the flash drive to safety. When I leave by the rear exit, and I intend to, I'm going to find a hiding place and make sure those two kidnappers don't go after you."

Sadie clasped her hands around his neck. "When this is over, we need to talk—about the future."

"Sadie, I've never stopped loving you."

THIRTEEN

Sadie pulled Brock's head toward hers and kissed him then murmured against his lips, "And I never stopped loving you. Stay alive."

Before he said anything else and took her focus away from getting help for Katie, Sadie released her embrace, spun around, and quickened her step toward the entrance into the cave. She leaned her upper body out of the opening as though scrutinizing her surroundings. When the tall "firefighter" spied her, she quickly ducked back into the cavern and grabbed the dog leash. "Let's go, Bella." She looked over her shoulder and saw the two men running toward her.

Sadie passed Brock, glanced at him, then started jogging down the main tunnel. She clicked on her flashlight when she could no longer see well in front of her. The twist and turns in the shaft might allow her to have her flashlight on some of the time with her hand partially covering the illumination. The rest of the time she slowed, ran her hand along the tunnel's wall, and followed the golden retriever, praying somehow they would all make it out alive.

"Bark, Bella."

Sadie glanced over her shoulder to see if she could tell where the two kidnappers were. So far it was dark behind her.

As she neared the underground chamber where the ground wasn't as smooth, coupled with the blackness, she was forced to use her flashlight more. She could barely hear the water dripping down from the ceiling because the sound of her heartbeat thudded against her ribcage.

Again, she commanded Bella to bark one last time halfway across the large room. The sound echoed off the stone walls. When she reached the other side, she paused to check behind her and catch her breath.

Where was Brock?

Where were the kidnap—

A gunshot blast reverberated through the air—followed by another one closer to her.

* * *

Brock waited at a turn in the shaft for the two men. He didn't want them to go back toward the entrance because of Simon and Katie. He needed to draw them deeper into the cavern.

When the kidnappers came into view, the glow from their flashlight made Brock's night vision goggles useless. He turned them off, and using the kidnappers' illumination, fired at the tall one. The bullet hit the stone wall near the man, and a piece of rock flew off and struck him in the arm. The guy stepped back.

His partner pulled his trigger then

ducked back around the curve, drawing the tall kidnapper with him.

As Brock neared the underground chamber, he put his night vision goggles back on. The rear exit wasn't too far from that room. He would make his stand there. That should give Simon and Katie as well as Sadie time to get out of the cave.

When he reached the underground chamber, he looked around as he ran toward a large stalagmite near the other end where Sadie had used to escape. He'd use the stone formation as a shield. He didn't want the two thugs near the tunnel where she was. He'd decided he would give Sadie as much time as he could because the rear exit was like a large pipe that she would have to crawl through to the end to reach the outside. He didn't want her or him getting caught in the tube with the kidnappers behind them. He didn't say anything to her about that because he didn't need her worrying about him. He needed Sadie to get help for her sister in case Simon couldn't.

Brock heard footsteps across the

cavern. The shorter assailant rushed into the large cavern, firing off shots rapidly one after the other. Brock ducked behind his barrier, watching through a hole in the stalagmite as the second man entered. Both of them had discarded part of their firefighter gear and attire. The shorter man went to the right. The tall kidnapper took the left side of the cavern.

As the tall thug came closer to Brock, he had to decide what to do. They weren't sure he and Sadie were in here. He hoped surprise was on his side because it was two to one at the moment.

* * *

The sound of gunfire, like a shootout, halted Sadie in her tracks as though a wave of icy air blew through and froze her. She wanted to go back and see if Brock was all right, but how could she help him? She didn't have a weapon. Brock could take care of himself. She had to get out of here and bring help.

The last thought propelled her forward

toward the pipeline, as she and Katie had named it when they were children and discovered it. Her sister wouldn't crawl into it until Sadie had and had returned to show Katie it was okay. As though Bella knew what Sadie's objective was, the dog tugged on her leash, drawing Sadie to the exit. As she stooped down with Bella next to her and shined her flashlight into the tunnel, silence reigned—no more barrage of bullets flying in the cavern.

That could mean Brock took care of the kidnappers, or they shot Brock. What if they all were lying on the stone floor wounded, needing help, or the two thugs or Brock were coming her way?

Bella took action and headed into the pipeline, making Sadie's decision for her. She crawled on her hands and knees toward the faint light ahead of her. Halfway to the end with the walls narrowing, she had to wiggle out of her backpack and push it forward. She released Bella's leash, so she could maneuver better and quicken her pace.

The quiet behind her caused her to

assume the worse. She had to get help and pray the two kidnappers were the only people after the flash drive.

I put my trust in You, Lord.

The light grew brighter as she neared the end of the pipeline. When she emerged, Bella approached her with her tail wagging. Sadie hugged her before she rose and looked around. Smoke hung in the air, making her eyes water, but she didn't see any flames. Off to the left about a couple of hundred yards, she spied two firefighters, different from the ones after her. As she moved toward them, she waved at them and yelled, "Help."

The two men quickly covered the distance between them. "Ma'am, are you okay? Where were you?"

She pointed back at the cave. "In the mine. Please call the sheriff and have him come right away with several deputies. There are two men, dressed as firefighters with guns in the mine searching for my sister and two friends." Her words rattled from her, and she wasn't even sure she was conveying the emergency situation adequately. "She's injured, and the others could be, too, by now. Let the sheriff know that Brock Carrington and his brother are in the mine protecting Katie Williams. We need help now."

"The entrance to the mine is that way." One of them pointed in the direction of the cave's main entrance. "Where did you come from?"

Sadie waved her hand toward the hole. "There's a back exit I used. It's not wide for big people." Which suddenly made Sadie realize that Brock probably couldn't escape that way.

After one of the firefighters reported the need for paramedics and law enforcement officers, Sadie started walking toward the cave's main entrance while she explained to the two men in detail what happened.

Halfway to the mine, the firefighter who called in the report received a message that the paramedics, Sheriff Maxwell, and his deputies were in the area and already there. Simon Carrington had contacted them.

Thankful Simon had been able to get

out of the cave before she had, Sadie exhaled a long sigh of relief. She hurried her pace with Bella by her side. The two men kept up with Sadie. She needed to see that Katie, Brock and Simon were all right, especially after all that gunfire.

When she reached the mine's entrance, paramedics were carrying Katie, with an oxygen mask over her face, out of the opening. Simon followed behind them. Sadie ran to them. "I'm here, Sis. Will she be okay? She has asthma as well as a bump on her head and a swollen ankle," she rambled until Simon clasped her upper arm and got her attention.

"I've already told them."

"Where's Brock?" Sadie asked as the paramedics continued down the slope. She needed to go with her sister, but she needed to know that Brock was all right. She was the one who dragged him into this.

The rat-a-tat of gunfire going off resounded through the main tunnel. She started for the underground chamber where Brock was last, but a deputy stopped her.

* * *

Brock peered through the small hole that allowed him to view the entrance to the large chamber at the end where the abductors were, as well as the most direct path to where Sadie went. The tall kidnapper hunkered down and ran in Brock's direction to a sizeable stone and hid behind it before he could get off a shot. The other man started to move forward like his partner. Anticipating it, Brock poked his head up above the stalagmite and squeezed off a round to alert the two kidnappers that he wouldn't let them pass him. The guy dove back behind the boulder where he'd been hiding.

After another five-minute standoff in the cavern, Brock shouted while watching through his peephole. "She's gone. So is the flash drive. You might as well give up. It's over."

The shorter kidnapper nearer the tunnel that led to the cave's opening darted toward it and ran into two deputies and Clay, their guns drawn. As one deputy handcuffed the assailant, the tall one rose behind his stone enough to let off a series of shots at the sheriff and deputies. "Clay!" Brock shouted a warning. He had a better sight of the shooter than law enforcement did. He popped up and shot the last kidnapper. The tall thug staggered forward and fell down onto the stone floor.

Brock called out once again to Clay and the other men while rushing the man and grabbing his weapon that had fallen from his hand when he was hit. When Brock saw Clay head toward him, he met him. "How're Sadie, Katie, and Simon?"

"I don't know about Sadie, but Katie is getting medical help, and Simon is fine. Go. I'll take care of these two."

Brock slung his rifle over his shoulder and ran toward the exit. Sadie had plenty of time to get out of the rear of the cave—unless something happened that he hadn't expected.

When he came close to the cave's entrance, he rounded the last curve in the tunnel and ran right into Sadie, with Simon and Bella a few steps behind her. Brock wrapped his arms around her and held her as though he would never let her out of his sight again. "You okay?"

She nodded against his chest. "Are you?"

"Yes, now that you're here and Katie is getting medical help." He bent his head forward and touched her forehead. "It's over. Clay's got the other two kidnappers. Let's go see how Katie's doing."

"That sounds great."

Brock kissed the top of her head then pulled away, slung his arm around her shoulder, and strode toward the exit. "We have a lot to talk about when this is over."

"Agreed. I won't feel safe until whoever is behind this flash drive is caught."

* * *

The next day, Brock pulled into Katie's driveway with both sisters in his car. He parked in front of the house, which had survived the wildfire along with his and her neighbor's place on the other side. After he climbed from Katie's Chevy sedan, found by two hikers in thick brush off the highway where Katie had hidden it in hopes the thugs after her thought she drove out of the area, he opened the back door to help Katie out of the vehicle. She scooted over to the edge of the seat, and he held up one crutch for her to stabilize herself when she exited. Then he handed her the second. "Okay?"

"Yes, now that I'm home. I'm just hoping the nightmare's over soon. When's Clay coming to let us know what's happening with the case?"

Brock chuckled as Sadie rounded the hood and stopped next to him. "Give him time. He probably hasn't even brought in Mr. Fox yet."

Sadie took his hand. "Let's go inside. I'll feel better when he's caught."

In the large cabin, Katie headed for her lounge chair and sat. "Is Simon cooking lunch?"

Simon stepped out of the kitchen. "No, that's dinner you're smelling. It's a pot roast slow cooking. I made ham sandwiches for lunch. I'll bring them out here, and you can grab one when you want. I'm taking Bella for a walk. I want to see the extent of the fire damage."

After Simon left, Sadie fixed a plate for Katie and brought it to her then sat next to Brock on the couch. "I'm staying here until you're feeling better."

"I'd love that after what has happened. Thanks for cleaning up the mess. After you told me those criminals trashed this place, I wasn't relishing cleaning it up with a fractured ankle." Katie leaned back in the chair and raised the footrest.

"You'll have to take it easy for a while. You have a concussion, too." Brock clasped Sadie's hand and held it. He never wanted to let it go, but with all that occurred yesterday, he and Sadie hadn't really had a chance to talk.

Katie sighed. "You don't have to remind me. My head is doing a good job of that." She took a bite of her sandwich. "I wish I'd never found those shipment slips and the money being put regularly into a bank account not tied to Mason and Fox. After trying to find the information in the company's accounting system, I put all the data I had on a flash drive and then went to Tom. I was hoping he had an explanation, but he didn't know either. He told me he would look into it. The chief financial officer had quit six months ago, and Tom thought he might know. The morning this all started, Tom called me and told me that the ex-CFO had disappeared. Tom couldn't find him, so he called Mr. Fox about the situation. That's why I went to see Tom, but instead I saw my boss being murdered."

"Why didn't they replace their CFO within that time?" Sadie snuggled closer to Brock.

"Tom was being groomed for that job but didn't have that official title yet. Mr. Fox was the owner that oversaw the finances, but he was rarely down on our floor."

"It could be several things—money laundering, embezzlement, or some kind of smuggling scheme. I hope Clay has some answers." Because Brock wanted his normal life back. As long as Katie could be in trouble, that meant Sadie could be, too.

After they finished their late lunch, Sadie took the dishes into the kitchen.

Brock followed her to make sure she was all right. "Katie's falling asleep. Everything's catching up with her. I thought I'd leave her there. I know she'll want to be here when Clay comes."

"Most definitely."

While Sadie rinsed off the plates, Brock put them in the dishwasher then shut its door. "These past several days have been full of a lot of emotions and danger." He stepped closer to Sadie, backing her up against the counter. "I learned a couple of things through this ordeal. One, the shots being fired at me didn't cause me to break down. I kept my thoughts on you and making sure you were protected. Two, not being a 'whole' man never interfered with what I needed to do to keep you safe. And three, I love you more than I ever did. I realize now that I made a terrible mistake four years ago. All I wanted to do was face my recovery alone. I didn't want others to see me struggling. I'd always been the strong one. Now, even more, I understand the gift of Bella. She taught me it was okay to need someone to help me recover."

"I love you, Brock. We'll face the bad—and the good—together." She locked her hands together behind his neck and drew him toward her. "Kiss me."

And he did with great pleasure. He poured himself into it, hoping to show her the depth of his feelings.

The doorbell rang and broke Sadie and him apart. She chuckled as she hurried toward the entrance. "Katie, stay there. I'll get it." She looked out the peephole and opened the door to Clay. "Come in. We've been eagerly waiting for you."

Brock joined Sadie and Clay. "It's good to see you. Let's sit in the living room."

When they were settled on the couch except for Katie across from them, Clay said, "All three of the kidnappers were eager to sell out Mr. Fox. He hired them to get the flash drive from either Connors or Katie, whoever had it. An FBI agent called in to help said it's a money laundering scam. It's essentially turning dirty money from things like selling drugs or smuggling humans into clean money that doesn't send up a red flag to the government."

Katie's face paled. "Mr. Fox is one of the owners of the company. Is Mr. Mason involved, too?"

"The FBI doesn't think so. They've been watching the company for the past six months and nothing has come up to indicate otherwise."

"Did the kidnappers start the wildfires?" Brock asked, slipping his arm along Sadie's shoulders.

"Not the first one but the one on this mountain. It was a good thing the wind changed slightly, or homes would have been destroyed, including both of yours."

Sadie relaxed against Brock. "It's nice to feel safe again. You should have just called us. You have to be tired after the past few days."

Clay stood. "I'm on my way home."

Brock laughed. "In a roundabout way." He rose and walked with Clay to the door.

After shaking the sheriff's hand, Brock waited for Simon and Bella to come into the house.

Brock held his hand out to Sadie. "Will you come over to my place? I have something I'd like to show you.

She crossed to the door and took his hand.

"I'll stay here in case Katie wants to go lie down upstairs." Simon looked at Sadie's sister. "I'll make sure you get to your bedroom safely."

Katie smiled. "I appreciate that. I'd rather sleep in my own bed. That's why I had people at the hospital show me how to use crutches on stairs."

Sadie glanced first at Simon then Katie. "Is something going on?'

"We're just going to my place." Brock ushered Sadie out the house.

"Brock Carrington, I know you, and you're up to something."

He kept going, and she followed him. When he arrived at his home, he went inside and left Sadie downstairs while he hurried up to the second floor and retrieved what he needed.

When he returned to the living room, he headed straight for the most beautiful person he knew. She meant everything to him. He knelt on his good leg, took a box out of his pocket, and opened it. "Will you marry me?"

"You kept the ring?" Sadie asked in a stunned voice.

"I couldn't get rid of it. I tried, but it just didn't feel right. You don't have to answer my question right away. But the ring is here whenever you want it."

She snatched the box from his hand. "I don't have to wait a day, an hour or another second. Yes, I want to marry you and soon."

He rose, plucked the one-carat, square diamond ring from the box, and slid it on her finger. "I hope you never take it off again."

"I love you." Sadie embraced him and kissed Brock.

"And I love you," he whispered against her lips and claimed them.

HUNTED

Book One in
EVERYDAY HEROES Series
by Margaret Daley

Murder. On the Run. Second Chances.

Luke Michaels' relaxing camping trip ends when he witnesses a woman being thrown from a bridge. He dives into the river to save her, shocked to find her wrapped in chains. As a canine search and rescue volunteer, Luke has assisted many victims, but never a beauty whose defeated gaze ignites his primal urge to protect. When Megan Witherspoon's killers make it clear they won't stop, Luke fights to save her, but can he keep her alive long enough to find out who is after her?

OBSESSED

Book Two in
EVERYDAY HEROES Series
by Margaret Daley

Stalker. Arson. Murder.

When a stalker ruthlessly targets people she loves, a woman flees her old life, creating a new identity as Serena Remington. Her plan to escape the madman and lead him away from family and friends worked for three years. Now he's back. With nowhere else to run, her only choice is war. Quinn Taylor, her neighbor and a firefighter with expertise in arson, comes to her aid, but will it be in time to save her?

DEADLY HUNT

Book One in
Strong Women, Extraordinary Situations
by Margaret Daley

All bodyguard Tess Miller wants is a vacation. But when a wounded stranger stumbles into her isolated cabin in the Arizona mountains, Tess becomes his lifeline. When Shane Burkhart opens his eyes, all he can focus on is his guardian angel leaning over him. And in the days to come he will need a guardian angel while being hunted by someone who wants him dead.

DEADLY INTENT
Book Two in
Strong Women, Extraordinary Situations
by Margaret Daley

Texas Ranger Sarah Osborn thought she would never see her high school sweetheart, Ian O'Leary, again. But fifteen years later, Ian, an ex-FBI agent, has someone targeting him, and she's assigned to the case. Can Sarah protect Ian and her heart?

DEADLY HOLIDAY
Book Three in
Strong Women, Extraordinary Situations
by Margaret Daley

Tory Caldwell witnesses a hit-and-run, but when the dead victim disappears from the scene, police doubt a crime has been committed. Tory is threatened when she keeps insisting she saw a man killed and the only one who believes her is her neighbor, Jordan Steele. Together, can they solve the mystery of the disappearing body and stay alive?

DEADLY COUNTDOWN
Book Four in
Strong Women, Extraordinary Situations
by Margaret Daley

Allie Martin, a widow, has a secret protector who manipulates her life without anyone knowing until...

When Remy Broussard, an injured police officer, returns to Port David, Louisiana to visit before his medical leave is over, he discovers his childhood friend, Allie Martin, is being stalked. As Remy protects Allie and tries to find her stalker, they realize their feelings go beyond friendship.

When the stalker is found, they begin to explore the deeper feelings they have for each other, only to have a more sinister threat come between them. Will Allie be able to save Remy before he dies at the hand of a maniac?

DEADLY NOEL

Book Five in
Strong Women, Extraordinary Situations
by Margaret Daley

Assistant DA, Kira Davis, convicted the wrong man—Gabriel Michaels, a single dad with a young daughter. When new evidence was brought forth, his conviction was overturned, and Gabriel returned home to his ranch to put his life back together. Although Gabriel is free, the murderer of his wife is still out there and resumes killing women. In a desperate alliance, Kira and Gabriel join forces to find the true identity of the person terrorizing their town. Will they be able to forgive the past and find the killer before it's too late?

DEADLY LEGACY
Book Seven in
Strong Women, Extraordinary Situations
by Margaret Daley

Legacy of Secrets. Threats and Danger. Second Chances.

Down on her luck, single mom, Lacey St. John, believes her life has finally changed for the better when she receives an inheritance from a wealthy stranger. Her ancestral home she'd thought forever lost has been transformed into a lucrative bed and breakfast guaranteed to bring much-needed financial security. Her happiness is complete until strange happenings erode her sense of well being. When her life is threatened, she turns to neighbor and police detective, Ryan McNeil, for help. He promises to solve the mystery of who's ruining her newfound peace of mind, but when her troubles escalate to the point that her every move leads to danger, she's unsure who to trust. Is the strong, capable neighbor she's falling for as amazing as he seems? Or could he be the man who wants her dead?

DEADLY NIGHT, SILENT NIGHT
Book Eight in
Strong Women, Extraordinary Situations
by Margaret Daley

Revenge. Sabotage. Second Chances.

Widow Rebecca Howard runs a successful store chain that is being targeted during the holiday season. Detective Alex Kincaid, best friends with Rebecca's twin brother, is investigating the hacking of the store's computer system. When the attacks become personal, Alex must find the assailant before Rebecca, the woman he's falling in love with, is murdered.

DEADLY FIRES
Book Nine in
Strong Women, Extraordinary Situations
by Margaret Daley

Second Chances. Revenge. Arson.

A saboteur targets Alexia Richards and her family company. As the incidents become more lethal, Alexia must depend on a former Delta Force soldier, Cole Knight, a man from her past that she loved. When their son died in a fire, their grief and anger drove them apart. Can Alexia and Cole work through their pain and join forces to find the person who wants her dead?

DEADLY SECRETS
Book Ten in
Strong Women, Extraordinary Situations
by Margaret Daley

Secrets. Murder. Reunion.

Sarah St. John, an FBI profiler, finally returns home after fifteen years for her niece's wedding. But in less than a day, Sarah's world is shattered when her niece is kidnapped the night before her vows. Sarah can't shake the feeling her own highly personal reason for leaving Hunter Davis at the altar is now playing out again in this nightmarish scene with her niece.

Sarah has to work with Detective Hunter Davis, her ex-fiancé, to find her niece before the young woman becomes the latest victim of a serial killer. Sarah must relive part of her past in order to assure there is a future for her niece and herself. Can Sarah and Hunter overcome their painful past and work together before the killer strikes again?

About the Author

Margaret Daley, a USA Today's Bestselling author of over 105 books (five million plus sold worldwide), has been married for over forty-seven years and is a firm believer in romance and love. When she isn't traveling or being with her two granddaughters, she's writing love stories, often with a suspense/mystery thread and corralling her cats that think they rule her household. To find out more about Margaret visit her website at www.margaretdaley.com.

Facebook:
www.facebook.com/margaretdaleybooks

Twitter:
twitter.com/margaretdaley

Goodreads:
www.goodreads.com/author/Margaret_Daley

Link to sign up for my newsletter on front page of website: www.margaretdaley.com